ERAMANE

ERAMANE

FRANKIE ASH

ARCHWAY
PUBLISHING

Archway Publishing books may be ordered through booksellers or by contacting:

Archway Publishing
1663 Liberty Drive
Bloomington, IN 47403
www.archwaypublishing.com
1-(888)-242-5904

ISBN: 978-1-4808-0179-0 (sc)
ISBN: 978-1-4808-0180-6 (e)

Library of Congress Control Number: 2013914379

Printed in the United States of America

Archway Publishing rev. date: 8/8/2013

THE CLiFF

WiND WHiPPED THROUGH KORA'S HAIR as she stood at the edge of the ocean cliff, her dress tattered and torn, legs scratched and bleeding from running through the briar patches in the woods. Normally she would be more careful when passing through the thorn brush, but Kora was desperate, and her life—never mind her legs and dress—meant nothing to her now. Kora's husband pursued her.

"Kora!" he shouted. "Stop! Please!" he pleaded while trying to reach her.

But Kora did not turn to face him. He ran as fast as he could, each step bringing him closer to his wife. Kora's husband stretched his arms out, reaching for her as he ran. He called to her again, "Kora!" But it was too late. *Swoosh*, she was gone. Kora made her choice, the choice to end her life and the life of the monster growing in her womb.

A BEAUTIFUL YOUNG COUPLE

"KALEB, THE FIRE IS DYING DOWN. Can you go bring in some more wood from outside?" Ramaya asked her husband as she knitted a white blanket. Kaleb was on the floor trying to hammer down a loose wooden floorboard. He looked up at his beautiful wife and smiled. She was sitting in a rocking chair with the hearth to her back. A warm, golden glow came from behind Ramaya, lighting up her long auburn hair. Kaleb stared for a moment, admiring her beauty. They were a beautiful young couple, married only two days ago. Ramaya was the daughter of a poor widower, and Kaleb was the son of a well-to-do farmer. They had met when Kaleb and his father traveled to her village to deliver goods for the small town.

Kaleb crawled over to his bride and sat up on his knees. "I would give you the world if you wanted, my love," he replied as he played with a lock of her hair.

"I already have it," Ramaya smiled as she stared into his bright green eyes. Kaleb leaned into his wife and pressed his lips to hers. Kaleb's passion for Ramaya seemed like it was going to get in the way of him getting the firewood, but Ramaya slowly pushed her husband away. "Kaleb, get the wood on the fire; our love alone will not keep us warm." Kaleb stood and kissed her on her head. As he stood there with his eyes closed, Ramaya could hear him take a deep breath, inhaling the scent of her hair, taking it in.

"I will be right back," he said as he walked to the door and put on his jacket and boots. He smiled at his lovely wife and stepped out.

The fire was down to small flames and hot coals, and Kaleb had not returned with more wood. Ramaya walked to the window to see what was taking him so long. Not seeing him from the window, she returned to her chair. She tried to continue knitting the blanket she was making for the winter, but she rose from the chair again, unsettled. She walked back to the window and leaned in close, putting her hands up to block her own reflection. Still she did not see Kaleb. Ramaya went to the front door and pulled her coat over her shoulders. She slipped her feet into her new slippers. Kaleb had purchased them for her from a neighboring village. They were very warm and lined with wool. Ramaya opened the door, and a gust of cold wind blew in on her. She quickly pulled the door shut and walked around the porch to the pile of firewood. Ramaya called for her husband. She was answered only by the wind blowing through the branches of the nearby trees. "Kaleb," she shouted loudly this time, worry in her voice. Not seeing her husband on the porch or in the side yard, Ramaya walked down the porch stairs to the yard and made her way to the back of the house. It seemed darker in the backyard, because the forest lined the house there. "Kaleb … please. This is not funny!" Ramaya shouted once more. Suddenly the winds ceased, and the air became thick with a fearful silence. A voice came from behind her.

"Ramaya," the deep voice spoke. Startled, she quickly turned, knowing this was not the voice of her husband. The silhouette of a man stood between the house and Ramaya. He walked closer to her. "I am not here to end your life, Ramaya. Your fate is not that of your husband." Ramaya's eyes darted around the yard for her beloved.

"Kaleb!" she shouted again, tears filling her eyes.

"He cannot hear you. His ears will not hear your voice again," the stranger said, pointing to the tall trees backing the yard. Ramaya looked in the direction he pointed and screamed in terror. Kaleb was pinned to one of the trees. Foliage wrapped around his torso, as if the tree were holding on to him. His face was expressionless; he looked as if he were in a trance. The stranger moved toward Kaleb. Ramaya watched as the man approached her incapacitated husband. Her eyes blinked rapidly, trying to adjust to what she was seeing as the stranger made his way to Kaleb. In disbelief, Ramaya watched the stranger transform into a beast, a frightening creature with horns and wings. The nine-foot-tall monster closed in on Kaleb and latched its enormous, taloned hands around his throat. Holding onto Kaleb's neck, the creature secured its other hand to the top of Kaleb's head. In one fast motion, the beast pulled Kaleb's body away from the tree, tossing it to the ground. It smacked with a solid thud, like an old rag doll that hits the ground after a pesky brother snatches it from his little sister's caring hands.

Looking back at Ramaya, who stood quivering at the sight of her husband's lifeless body, the beast said, "He will make a great harvest." Ramaya turned her attention back to the fiend, and what she saw jolted her more than anything she had witnessed already; the beast still held something against the trunk of the tall tree. Beneath the grip of the otherworldly beast stood a soft, whitish-gray, ghostly image, Kaleb's soul. The fiend placed its palm on the soul's chest and began to harvest. A faint glow moved out of the soul and up the arm of the creature, making its way through the beast's entire body. The creature was illuminated by its harvest; it beamed like waters hit by the light of a full moon. Ramaya watched on, helpless, numb with fear and astonishment, as the beast slowly drained her husband. When Kaleb's soul no longer emanated any light, the creature retracted its hand, and what remained of Kaleb's essence vanished into the air.

The creature stood for a brief moment, letting its harvest disperse throughout its body. Its chest rose as it inhaled and then lowered in an exhalation of gratification. Then the creature began to distort, and human features emerged. The beast, now fully human, approached Ramaya and pulled her to him. Despite her efforts to break free, he wrapped her up in his arms and whispered in her ear. "Eovettzi˜ nomistara." He repeated the words in a soft, soothing tone until Ramaya calmed and fell into a trancelike state, no different than the state Kaleb was in when he was bound to the tree. This stranger had great power, his words like an intoxicant, and no human had a chance to escape his will.

The stranger released his hold on Ramaya; she remained motionless. The man placed his hands on each side of Ramaya's face, holding her gaze on him. He leaned into her and touched his lips to hers. A small orb of yellow light passed from his mouth to hers; it moved down her throat and settled in her belly.

"I will return for my son," he said softly in her ear while she remained lifeless in his grasp. "Give life to my child, and I will return to relieve you of this burden; I will restore your life as it was before this night. You will have your husband again." Tears of agony, despair, and hope ran down Ramaya's face as he spoke of returning Kaleb to her. Ramaya would give birth to a thousand of his children to have her husband back.

A Child Is Born

STORM CLOUDS SETTLED OVER THE small village where Ramaya lived. Their dark, heavy plumes would usher in the fiend that had taken Kaleb from his wife. The child on which Ramaya so greatly depended to ensure the return of her husband would arrive soon, and when the shadow of night descended, it would bring the dreadful beast with it.

Ramaya's bedroom was small, and it strained to contain Ivan, Kaleb's father, and the housemaid. Ramaya lay waiting to give birth; her labor pains became more frequent, and her breaths more rapid.

"Get her some water," ordered Ivan. The sound of thunder intruded on his words. A timid young woman scurried to get Ramaya something to quench her thirst.

"How can you let this happen? He is your son, Ivan!" Ramaya protested the plan of Cole and his men to keep the child from its father. "If you take him, then I will not get

6

my husband back!" Ramaya screamed through her labor pains.

"I understand, child. We have discussed this many times," Ivan said, "but you cannot count on this to be true. How can we trust the words from the Nameless One?" he asked, not intending for her to answer.

"We have to try; please do not take the baby!" Ramaya pleaded.

"Do you not think that I have considered this a thousand times, Ramaya? Yes, he was my son, and I miss him dearly, but this child is special, Ramaya. He needs to be raised as one of us. If these men fail to destroy the Nameless One tonight, we will need this child to do what they could not. Do you not understand this?"

"I understand that you are going to keep me from my beloved." Ramaya's voice faded to a whimper; she knew that Ivan, Cole, and the men in the next room would never allow the Nameless One to leave with its child. She realized that she would never see Kaleb again.

Kaleb's murder was rumored throughout the lands neighboring Ramaya's hometown. A short time after his death, another stranger visited Ramaya; this one came to help. His name was Cole, and he was hunting Kaleb's attacker. He explained to Ramaya how he'd lost his wife because of the fiend. Cole told her that his wife could not bear the thought of growing a child in her that belonged to what she believed was a demon.

"She threw herself over the ocean cliff," he explained, his tone solemn. "I have been searching for this creature since the day my wife died a little more than ten years ago."

Cole retold Ramaya stories of the beast that he had heard along his travels. "Most people believe that the myth of a flying demon is just that, a myth. But those few that have laid eyes on the creature know the extent of its power, and they are fearful. Those folks, the ones who have seen it, call it the Nameless One," he said. "They say he is a demon that escaped from the dark world to roam our lands freely."

After hearing Ramaya's story, Cole knew that he was dealing with the same creature, the one responsible for his wife's death. "I do not know why the fiend changes into a human form, but the only stories of the creature transforming have to do with him passing that yellow light into women. There have only been three that I know of: my wife, a young woman who was hanged by her own people, and you."

In the decade since his wife's death, Cole had searched relentlessly for the beast. Not once had he ever been so close to actually seeing the monster with his own eyes as he would be tonight. Cole knew the beast would come for the child. As far as he knew, Ramaya was the only woman to have carried the fiend's child to its full term. But the Nameless One was crafty and unpredictable. There never seemed to be a specific time of the night when it would attack—it just came. But this night Cole waited in eager anticipation, for he truly believed that he, and the men he had gathered, would stand a chance of defeating the beast and freeing the land and its people of the monstrosity.

A small brigade of ten men gathered around the hearth in Ramaya's home. Six were dressed alike: leather pants, long-sleeved shirts, and black cloaks with hoods. Each man also had a satchel just large enough to secure and transport a new-born. A low, steady tone of voices floated about the room as each man discussed his thoughts on the Nameless One. One of them tossed a small cut of wood into the fire, rustling up the embers.

"Get those ashes out of the fire and cooled. We cannot use them if they are hot," Reeve ordered. "Here, take these and soak up as much birthing waste as you can," Reeve continued as he tossed several rags to the woman aiding Ramaya, who was now only moments away from birthing the child. The men knew the nameless fiend would soon arrive, and each held a firm grasp on his weapon.

"The baby is coming!" Ramaya shouted as she began to bear down in pain. Her screams of childbirth were matched with the angry winds that beat against her home. It did not take her long to deliver the son of the Nameless One. Ramaya looked over the child while the housemaid wiped it down. The hefty baby boy favored his mother, and Ramaya noticed it right away. But she wanted nothing to do with the child, since she knew these men would not let the creature take him, and they would not let her keep him. Ivan explained to her that the fiend may have a link with her, and that if she were to reunite with her child, the beast might be able to locate them. She would not get to be a mother to the baby boy, so she turned her head to keep from viewing the child.

"Take it!" she shouted at the woman holding the baby. "Get it away from me!" she screamed. The young woman bundled the child in blankets and handed it to Ivan. He was to take the child and ride as fast as he could to the caves of a

nearby mountain range. A trusted friend, a man with mod-
erate talents of magic, a man capable of raising such a special child would be waiting to take the infant to a secret place
where the Nameless One could not find him.

"He grew in your belly, Ramaya; remember that. This
child will not grow to be like his father. He will be a pure
spirit, just like his mother. The FateSeers have revealed this
to us, and they are never wrong," Ivan said, trying to console her. "That beast cannot bring our Kaleb back. Not the
Kaleb we knew and loved. He would not be the same—just a
body without a soul, Ramaya," Ivan said as he approached her.
"Give the child your blessing before we part," he suggested,
holding out the child to her.

"Please, I cannot bear to look at him," Ramaya wept, and
her voice trembled.

Ivan took the child to Reeve, who smeared ash on the
child's skin to mask the newborn's scent. "You must go now,"
Cole commanded. He gave rags covered in afterbirth to each
of the men. They stuffed them into their satchels. Cole's hope
was to distract the demon, with these riders bearing the scent
of the child. These men would dispatch in different directions,
and Ivan would be able to reach the cave with the child.

The night was at its peak, and Cole, Reeve, and the rest of the
men who were not part of the distraction were prepared for
an encounter with the Nameless One. Thunder rumbled and
a bright bolt of lightning illuminated the darkness—and the

entrance of the Nameless One, the beast Cole had waited so long to see.

The winged creature burst through the door, ripping it away from the structure of the house. It landed with a calculated thud and did a rapid scan of the room, looking for its child, but the distributed smell of the afterbirth puzzled the fiend, confusing it. Ivan and the six men who were to ride off with him were unable to disperse before the fiend arrived, and now the beast was blocking their only exit. The creature was massive, the size of several men. Black, leathery-looking skin covered the beast like impenetrable chain mail. Its eyes burned a fierce yellow-orange, and giant horns protruded out from its brow, turning back and coiling down by its ears, as if to cover its head like a helmet. A long mane of silver hair parted the horns and draped halfway down the beast's massive back.

"Where is my son?" screamed the Nameless One, continuing to sniff and scan the room as it made its way to Ramaya. She sat up in a futile attempt to defend herself.

"He is dead. He lasted only a moment after birth and then died," she said faintly, terrified by the beast. The frightful creature grabbed her by her throat and demanded the whereabouts of its son once more. Even if she'd wanted to speak the truth, the brute had too strong of a grip; she could not breathe. Cole hurried to defend her, shooting an arrow in the beast's lower back. The Nameless One released Ramaya and rushed Cole, pinning him to the ground. The crushing weight of the colossal creature forced the air from Cole's lungs, and he lost consciousness. A man with a wooden pail tossed a liquid mixture on the back of the beast. The Nameless One paused for a moment to examine the greasy liquid. It ran its fingers in the oily substance and brought them up to his nose. Then it smiled at the man with the empty pale. The beast yanked drapes from the window pane and used them to wipe some of the liquid off. Nearby a man plunged a small tree limb into the embers of the hearth, igniting the cloth tethered to its end. He was unsteady and frightened by the surprising might of the Nameless One. With desperate aim, the man tossed the torch at the beast and struck his doused target.

Fire engulfed the creature's lower back and parts of its legs, places where the drapes had missed the splattered liquid. For a moment, the Nameless One dropped to its knees, the flames and black smoke temporarily dazing it. While the creature scrambled to rise, Ivan, Reeve and the remaining men bolted from the home, hoping that their plan to trick the fiend would still work. They ran out of the house and mounted their frightened horses. Gaining control of the steeds, the men dispersed in separate directions.

The inflamed demon jumped straight up, busting a hole in the roof of the small house. The flames continued to burn on parts of the beast's back and legs, and it screamed in frustration, sending an echo of its anger into the wilderness. As the Nameless One headed for a nearby pond, it scanned the area for the riders … locating each of them. The creature approached the pond and dove down into it and back up into the air again, flames extinguished. It sniffed for the scent of its child, only to locate it in all directions. The Nameless One headed for the nearest rider, who struggled to keep his horse in control. The beast grabbed the rider from his horse and saw that he was carrying only rags containing the scent of its creation. "Ahhhh!" the rider screamed as the beast brought him up to its face.

"Where is my son?"

"I ... I do not ... *ahhhhh*!" The man could not finish his words before the Nameless One gripped his head and tossed him in the air. The creature took flight again and sought a second man. This time it took a bit longer, as the men had entered the protection of the thick forest. Unfortunately for this man, he'd reached a sparse area where the forest thinned out a bit and made it easier for the Nameless One to seek him out. It swooped down and speared the rider off of his stallion, sending him to the earth. The rider bounced across the ground as if he were a stone skipping across the water. The fiend grabbed the man during his ground rolls and slung him against a tree. "Where are they taking my son?" the beast asked calmly as its breath penetrated the lungs of the battered rider. The man had suffered a deep laceration across his eye and was close to losing consciousness.

"Kill me. I will not tell you, demon," the brave man stated. At that moment, the creature knew it would not locate the child; too many men for the beast to track had left Ramaya's home and darted in separate directions. Now they were in the forest, and the Nameless One could not see them from the air. The scent had grown faint, and the beast could barely smell anything more than the blood oozing from the rider pinned against the tree. Lacking the desire to end the life of the severely injured rider, the Nameless One loosened its grip and let him fall to the ground, leaving him there to die slowly and painfully.

Twenty years After...

CHAPTER TWO

ERAMANE

IT IS A SUNNY DAY. Sounds of laughter and celebration fill the village of Eludwid. The quaint town bursts with excitement as festivities move through the streets like a fast breeze from the ocean. Lord Emach Danius has brought his men home from a victorious battle just in time for Autumn Blossom, the yearly jubilee. Eludwid's Autumn Blossom festival began many years ago. The celebration received its title because of the redtail flowers that turn the fields into flames. They blossom at the end of summer when the other flowers have lost their blooms. All of the surrounding villages come together to celebrate Autumn Blossom. Young ladies flit about, hoping to catch the eye of a hopeful sweetheart, while others reunite with their loved ones from neighboring villages. The season is changing, and though the days have been warm, the nights get cold enough to warrant the warmth of a beloved.

Near the apothecary, in an open area of grass, eager children are preparing to compete in a sack race. The first prize is a small, wooden, hand-carved trinket: a mountain cat, the territories' symbol, or a horse. "On three!" shouts a plump, red-faced woman. "One, two, three!" She smacks two round wooden discs together to sound the start of the sack race. Each contestant steps inside of the brown sack laid out in front of him or her and jumps up and down, making a run for the finish line. I make a weak effort to win. After all, I am competing against small children; my little friend Olli asked that I join in. I make sure to stay behind Olli; he is in last place, except for me. He tries with all of his might to keep jumping, but the day is at its hottest, and Olli feels it, mostly because of a prolonged period of an empty belly. His feet tangle inside of the sack, and he falls to the ground. *Thump*! I make a few more hops to reach him.

"Are you okay, Olli?" I ask. I am truly concerned for him. From where I was, he looked like he had taken a hard fall.

"I'm fine," he says, disappointed by his not finishing the race.

"Do not worry about it. Those wooden toys are not that great anyway. If you play with them too much, they will break," I say, trying to lift his spirits. I look up at the other contestants in time to see a girl in braids cross the finish line first. She squeals in victory, her braids smacking her face and shoulders as she jumps up and down.

"Yeah, but I wanted one," he says plainly. I understand his desire for the wooden toy; I once yearned for one as well, and my brother, Samiah, made sure he beat everyone in the race so that I got it, a mountain cat.

"Well, you know what, Olli?"

He looks at me through dull gray eyes. "What, Eramane?" he mumbles.

"I think that you are a fantastic competitor! You deserve a prize just as much as the rest of them. Come on," I say, "let us fetch you one." His eyes light up, and a crooked smile brightens his face, even through the dirt smudges. We stand from the grass and make our way to the prize basket. "Good morning, sir," I say to the toothless old man sitting on a stump and tending to the prize basket. "Did you make these?" I ask.

"Yes, m'lady. With these steady hands," he laughs and holds out his trembling fingers.

"They are lovely," I say reaching for a toy. "May I?"

"Yes, yes."

"Are they for sale?" I know they are not; they are just prizes for the children. But asking has excited the old man.

"You want to purchase one of these?" His laugh sounds like a whistle my brother taught me to make. It requires you to pull your lips in over your teeth, stick two fingers in the sides of your mouth, and blow. It is a sharp noise and can be soft or loud, depending on how hard you blow. The old man's whistles are sharp, probably because he has no teeth.

"Will you accept this for payment?" I hold out one coin stamped with a bird holding a leaf in its claw. It is more than enough for the toy. I could purchase every toy in the basket and much more with the coin.

"No, m'lady. That is too much. I cannot accept it. Please, just take one," he says.

"I insist," I say, placing the coin on top of a mountain cat that still remains in the basket. "Thank you. Good day, sir," I say and hand the toy to Olli, watching his eyes widen. I hear faint murmurs of disbelief from the old man as Olli and I walk away.

"A mountain cat!" Olli shouts. "Thanks, Eramane."

"Now that you have your wooden toy, how about we get something to eat? If that tummy of yours shrinks any more, your trousers might slide right off." We walk up the middle road of Eludwid, where all of its merchants are located. I want to take Olli to the breadmaker's. A fresh, hot honey loaf with some citrus water would be a delicious snack, and a filling one.

My belly is full; Olli's belly was bulging when I sent him off to fetch his mother. "Give this to your mother," I say handing Olli a satchel of bread loaves and another of cured meats. "And give these to her as well." I drop two coins in his hand and fold his fingers around them. I bend down to look him in the eyes. "You tell your mother to fetch me if the family needs food … anything. I will always be here to help you and yours, you understand?" Olli nods his head and gives me an enormous smile; he darts off and is out of sight in an instant. If he had shown that much speed in the race, he would have won.

I lean against a tall tree that throws a large shadow over the field where the games are held. The festival seemed more elaborate when I was younger. I remember the town's center would be filled with so many people that the field where I stand now would be speckled with temporary shelters for our neighboring visitors. Year by year, the speckled field has displayed fewer and fewer shelters. My parents say that the festival dwindles because more people are traveling to other lands in search for more rich soils, and that eventually the festival may not take place at all.

I am watching the townspeople mingle when my mother approaches me with a mischievous look.

"My dear Eramane," she gushes as she drapes herself around me, her eyes wild with excitement. "What are you doing over here by yourself, my darling?" My mother's smile is playful, and I immediately sense that she is up to something. "Do you know that Lebis is over by the blacksmith's back door, completely exhausted, waiting for that old goat Whiney to relieve him of his duties? You should go take him something refreshing to drink, Eramane."

"Oh, Mother," I exclaim. "You know as well as anyone not to disturb someone when they are working." I try desperately to avoid the conversation. Lebis always works very hard. Most of the time he is outside at the anvil, hammering away, and I cannot help but look at him every time our carriage passes Whiney's shop. The old man who owns the shop is always complaining about his aches and pains, so when we were children we nicknamed him Whiney. Even my mother took up calling him Whiney, because, she said, it suits him perfectly. His true name is Percival, but I have not heard anyone call him that in years. My mother noticed that Lebis caught my eye several weeks ago, and she has been poking her nose in ever since. *Why did she have to see me gawking at him?*

"Well, your father is worried that you will never marry, and we will be the family with the poor, pathetic, unwed daughter," my mother blurts out, and we both burst into laughter. She hugs me tightly. "Stay with me forever, my dearest Eramane. I do not mind," she whispers in my ear while she fluffs the back of my hair. She pulls me in, kisses my forehead, and walks away to fetch my father. Again I am alone, and now I am thinking about Lebis.

My brother, Samiah, is nuzzling his wife, Mira, on the breadmaker's stoop. They are watching the small parade between moments of laughter and kisses. Mira's long lavender dress makes her look like a flower, recently bloomed. Her golden hair is braided in a knot on top of her head. I suppose Samiah is saying playful things to her, because she keeps blushing and giggling. Mira's face flushes each time he whispers something in her ear. They were married last spring and have been trying for children, but Mira has yet to be with child. Several months ago, she and Samiah visited the FateSeer. She told them that a child will come and to be patient. My parents went to the FateSeer once. After they had Samiah, they were blessed with a second child. But at three months of pregnancy, my mother lost the baby. When she found out that she was pregnant with me, she and my father sought the knowledge of the FateSeer. The woman told them that they would have a girl, and that she would have a great gift. I always laugh when I think about that prophecy; I have no special gifts, unless one considers my embroidery. I once made a blanket with a scene of all the territories on it. I gave it to Lord Emach Danius as a birth celebration gift. My birth celebration recently passed;

I turned seventeen. My parents gave me a beautiful dress, and Mira gave me a beautiful glove set.

Mira is a wonderful lady. She and I spend a lot of time together, especially when Samiah is off with the Riders. She told me how she cried when Samiah proposed, that she never thought he would ask so soon. "In just four days, Eramane!" she said. She told me how he was nervous and how his sandy blond curls jiggled while he looked up at her, how the scar on the palm of his hand made it even easier to say yes. Samiah loves Mira; he has since the day her family moved to town six winters ago.

I walk up the breadmaker's steps to greet my brother and Mira. It makes me happy to see him enjoying himself. Much of the time he is serious and focused on his duty, always discussing ways to keep peace in our lands. Samiah commands Lord Danius's men, a privilege never held by someone so young. Before he joined with our uncle Karmick, he trained with swordsmen from all over. He seemed to know his destiny and was simply preparing himself, honing his skills. But when we were children, he would chase me around with dead insects or small, unfortunate animals, laughing all the while. I have many great memories of us as children.

"Eramane!" Mira exclaims and wiggles out of Samiah's gentle embrace. She rushes to me and hugs me tight. We trade a kiss on the cheek too.

"Hello, Mira. Are you two enjoying the festival?" I ask.

"Oh, is it not such a beautiful day to celebrate!" Mira looks back to Samiah, who smiles at her excitement. He extends his arms, inviting me in for an embrace. I hug him tightly; it is always an enormous relief when he returns home safe. After a quick, heartfelt hug, he pushes me away.

"Here, I had this made for you," he says, holding out a hairpin in the shape of a bird's wing. "I am sorry I was not here for your birth celebration."

"It is beautiful," I say, looking at the silver hairpin. I place it in my hair, above my ear. "How does it look?"

"Beautiful," Mira says, smiling at her husband. "It looks perfect there, Eramane." I hug Samiah again and thank him for the hairpin.

"Well, I am going to make my way back home. I need to gather some things before coming to stay with you two tomorrow," I say, walking back down the steps.

"Tell our parents to be safe," Samiah says.

"I will. See you tomorrow afternoon." I wave goodbye and follow the road leading to our home.

As I walk, I think about the day and all the people happily celebrating with their families. Yet in the midst of all this excitement, I cannot move beyond my boredom. I feel that there is something more out there, beyond Eludwid. Something exciting awaits me—something meaningful. I want to ride along with my brother to those distant lands I have only heard about. I want to meet a sorcerer. Nahmas met a fire summoner for the first time when he was a boy. I heard him telling my brother about it. Nahmas said that when he was a child, he and his two brothers were orphaned by an attack on their homeland. The young boys wandered through the forest for several days before stumbling upon a small army of men, not knowing they were the same men who had attacked their home. These men

caught the boys and were going to execute them without hesitation. But before they could raise a sword to the boys' necks,
a man holding fire in his hands appeared and set every man
in that army ablaze. Quicker than the brothers could blink,
the men were defeated and they were saved. I asked Samiah if
there was truth in Nahmas's story, and he said, "He is a trusted
Rider, Eramane, and he is not the only man with this story.
His two brothers will tell it to you the same."

I am fortunate, though, to be seventeen and unwed. I
have never even been courted by anyone. I have my family
to thank for this. They have declined four proposals. They
do not believe that a girl should marry someone she does not
know and cannot possibly love. My mother was promised to a
man much older than herself. She would cry herself to sleep at
night; she would beg her father to undo the engagement. She
was in love with another man, my father. Three days before the
wedding, her soon-to-be husband fell ill. He did not recover,
so my grandfather allowed her to marry her true love. She has
told me this story many times.

As I walk by Whiney's, I hear the familiar banging that
echoes from the anvil. I stop and watch as Lebis strikes a piece
of iron. He is handsome, but I would never admit that to my
mother. While I stand here, thoughts bouncing around in my
head, I notice Lily making her way over to Lebis. She twirls
her finger in her black, curly hair. She says something, getting
Lebis's attention, but I cannot hear her words. He looks up,
and a slight smile smoothes his rugged appearance. He says
something back. What are they saying? I walk a bit closer, trying to remain unnoticed. Still I cannot hear them. Lily speaks

again—her manner changes. Is she upset? It seems as though she is. Lily walks off hastily; Lebis turned her away! I cannot hide the smirk on my face. I remove it at once when I notice that Lebis is looking directly at me. He smiles and then returns to his work. Did he know I was here the entire time? *Humiliated* is not a strong enough word to describe how I feel. I turn and walk away, and then the smirk returns. My mother knows me too well. Of course I like Lebis; why would I not? He is handsome, he works hard, and, most importantly, he sent Lily away. But how am I ever going to get to know him if I am too nervous to speak to him? I have had a few chances to speak with him, but all I can summon is a whisper of a "hello," and that is it. What should I do? Maybe I should walk over to Lebis and give him a big kiss in front of everyone in the village. That would really be entertaining. To see the look on everyone's face, especially my brother's! No—I decide to keep walking.

It is evening now, and I should have been home long ago, but the festival kept my attention today. Each time I would pass a merchant I could not help but stop by and examine their goods. Last year I found a beautiful ring that I bought for my mother. She wears it every day. Not long ago, she thought that she lost it, and she cried for an entire morning. My father saved the day when he walked in the house with the ring in his hand. "What was your ring doing in Lady's stall?" My mother had taken it off before brushing Lady the previous evening. We have caretakers to tend the house and animals, but my mother always likes to brush her horse. It is a pleasure I enjoy too.

The streets have been abandoned after the excitement of the day. They emit a feeling of peace as I walk along them.

I like being in town when it is quiet. It gives me a chance to appreciate its beauty, without interruption by others. Most times, before Samiah was married, girls would rush up to me to inquire about him. Other folks want to know when my brother will be taking their sons, fathers, or husbands from them and into battle. I always give them a caring smile and a vague reply of "any day now" if the Riders are expected to return, and "soon" if they are expected to depart.

Most everyone has gone home to prepare for dinner, except those who are not ready to end the festivities; they are gathered on the mountaintop, having a wonderful time, I am sure. I am also sure that Mira and Samiah are on the mountaintop. My mother and father are likely to be at home, packing for their trip to the surrounding villages to sell grains and other goods. This is a trip my parents commonly make, and recently I have not accompanied them. I have been staying with Samiah and Mira while they are gone. Sometimes it is just Mira and me when Samiah is out protecting our lands, but he will be home for a few weeks and will not be leaving for another mission until our parents return. I heard him tell Father this earlier today.

I make my way to the crest of the large hill that spills down to our stone home, nestled against the forest. The great-house is large enough for several families, but only the three of us live here. My father inherited it from his father; it has been in the Fahnestock family for six generations. A smaller stone house sits across the meadow. Our caretakers live there. They are a family of seven: father and mother; two sons, ages fifteen and eleven; and three daughters, ages sixteen, nine, and seven.

Fields of farm land and rolling hills that sprout with wild-flowers in the spring push out from around our house. I am walking down the hill and see that my father is loading luggage on the carriage. Nearing the horse carriage, I hear my father shout, "Alora, is that all of them?" He looks up and sees my grin. "It is as if she does not expect to ever return home," he says as he hops down from the carriage. He walks over and hugs me. "I should go ahead and warn you," he says stepping back, still holding my shoulders. "Your mother has asked Lebis over to ..." He is interrupted.

"Randall!" Mother exclaims. She has a disapproving look on her face that reminds me of when she caught me play-acting a swordfight with a long, crooked stick and a tree.

"You have asked Lebis over to ... what?" I ask.

"I asked Lebis to stop by this evening to check our carriage wheels before we leave in the morning," she says.

"Why would father need to warn me about ..." Before I finish my words it occurs to me; she has arranged for Lebis and me to meet! I am not appreciative of this arrangement. It has caught me off guard; and, worst of all, he spotted me staring at him earlier today.

"Mother," I say, "I do not need you to arrange this for me. I spoke to him today already." I try to be convincing by standing up straight and smiling, "We have a date tomorrow," I say and turn toward the stables. "I will be in the stables—brushing Lady."

The sun is setting, spreading a red sheet across the sky. Lady is well groomed by now; her coat is shiny and fewer hairs are gathering in the brush. Oriana is tossing grain to the chickens that walk about freely. She told me several days ago that she favors a young man employed within Lord Danius's household. She is quiet this evening, which causes me to believe she has been turned away by her prince.

"Did you enjoy the festival today, Oriana?"

"Yes, m'lady." Oriana is timid in her reply.

"Oriana, you do not need to address me as 'my lady.' We are friends, are we not? Please address me as Eramane, always." I give her a smile to show my sincerity.

"Nealyn said I was but a servant, and that I should never expect to be anything more than a servant. He said that you should not be filling my head with fairy tales, and hopes of finding a prince."

"He has no business speaking to you in that manner, Oriana. I am making a trip into town in a few days; I will have words with him." Oriana does not seem to be uplifted by this. I walk around Lady and out of her stall. Oriana stands motionless, still grasping the empty grain pail. I wrap my arms around her and give her a squeeze. "You are not a servant, Oriana. You are my friend, and I love you. He said those things only because he is an ignorant boy. Real men do not treat ladies in such a manner." I squeeze her again. "You will find a prince one day, Oriana, I promise." I mean those words with all of my soul; if Oriana does not deserve true love, no one does.

We send the horses out to graze in the pasture for the night, so they do not need tending to, unless we get a storm. Then I will be up in the middle of the night chasing down frightened horses. I decide to leave them out anyway. Oriana and I walk back from the stables; she seems to have a renewed hope after we spoke more. I help Oriana finish the chores my mother asked of her, put the linens away, and arrange freshly picked flowers in a vase. Our mother is always picking flowers for the house. She says the flowers bring charm to the house and that such a large home needs a lot of charm.

Samiah and Mira are still out celebrating, yet I can sense that Mother was hoping for them to stop in for a visit. Not only is it Autumn Blossom, but Samiah and the Riders have been home for only a couple of days after being away for half of the year. Lord Danius sent Samiah and seventy other Riders to protect a village to the south. These undertakings were confidential and made sure to be discussed about privately. Samiah told me about this plot. He confessed to me his doubts of their safe return. Samiah explained to me that a clan named the Torbiuns was riding through the southern villages and killing anyone unfortunate enough to meet up with them. This clan had good reason to be feared, for it was rumored that they had a shadow caster. This was also when Samiah revealed to me that Nahmas, and his brothers, Terrin and Aurick were trace casters; when they traced, they could make their bodies almost invisible, and for this reason my brother named the three brothers the Ghosts. Nahmas said that the fire summoner who saved them when they were boys took them in as his own. He raised them, and he taught them the craft. It is unusual that each brother possesses the ability to cast, let alone the same casting ability, and this trait makes them exceptional.

The rumor of the Torbiuns possessing a shadow caster was false, and Samiah and the Riders reduced the clan to only a handful. The Riders protected the village and helped the townspeople build barriers in case of future invasion.

Samiah is courageous, yet our mother weeps each time he departs, for she is consumed with worry for her son. Samiah did not have to serve Lord Danius, but he chose to follow in our uncle's footsteps. Uncle Karmick used to serve as the commander of Lord Danius's forces, but three winters ago, Uncle Karmick was attacked in the night, while the Riders slept, by a force that no one could describe; it acted too swiftly for any of the men to see. None of Uncle Karmick's Riders could help him, because the creature took him up into the endless, dark night. His sword fell to the ground, and no one saw him again. Many of his Riders believed it to be some kind of creature that was summoned by an insane lord to the west. Lord Cavok was evil and wanted to rule every land in existence. Later Samiah, and the Riders he now commands, dismantled most of Lord Cavok's forces and drove him into faraway lands. He had no special powers of summoning frightening creatures. He was only a crazed man seeking power. I often think about what happened to my uncle and wonder if he really was taken away by some flying creature.

My parents have gone to bed early this evening; they will leave for their travels before the sun rises. I have gathered my mother's wool blanket and have snuggled down into my father's brown leather chair that sits close to the hearth. I am reading a book about a young man's brave search for his lost love. The heat from the fire has made the chapter about the dragon more vivid, and I find that I have scooted myself to the edge of the chair farthest from the hearth while I read of dragon fire consuming a small village. I am almost to the end of the chapter when I hear a tap at the door. I stand up from the chair and listen for a moment as I wonder what to do; I know who is there knocking. Making my way to the front door, I hesitate before opening it.

"Good evening," Lebis says. "My apologies for disturbing you so late this evening, but your mother asked that I stop by to inspect the carriage wheels." He is still dirty from working all day, but that does not matter; the dirt does not conceal his charm. I clear my throat.

"They have gone to bed, but the carriage is just there." I point to the loaded-down carriage in the front of our home. I am unexpectedly more nervous than usual. I can feel myself perspiring, and this only makes me more anxious.

"Yes, I see it there," he says. "Would you mind holding a lantern for me while I take a look?" I hesitate. "It is just that it is dark, and I am afraid to be out here all alone," he says with a wide smile. I laugh and step outside, closing the front door behind me. Lebis pulls a lantern from a satchel hanging from his horse.

"She is beautiful. What is her name?" I ask.

"Kelwyn."

"When did you purchase her? I have not seen her at Whin … I mean Percival's."

"You do not have to call him Percival on my behalf; he does complain most of time. 'Whiney' is appropriate," he says, another broad smile stretching across his face. "And what horse have you seen me with?"

His question embarrasses me. Is he admitting that he knows I look for him when I am in town? I change the subject.

"What did you make today" I ask, holding the light near the center of the carriage wheel.

"I worked most of the day on a sword."

"What kind of sword?" We move to the next wheel.

"A long one," he says.

"Do you think I would not know the difference?" Lebis stands up from the carriage wheel.

"No, Eramane, I am sure you would know the difference. I only meant that the sword was insignificant. The man I made it for only wanted it as display in his lodge. He was from a neighboring village and was leaving town this evening, so I had to work fast. That is all."

"I see. My brother has taught me all about swords, how to hold them, what sizes are the best in certain circumstances. Do you make his swords?"

"Yes," he says.

"So you know my brother well?"

"Yes." Our conversation stalls for a moment. "You look lovely; your dress is very pretty," Lebis says, his eyes focusing on a wheel mechanism.

"Thank you. Your mother made it. My mother and I purchase all of our clothing from her. She sews the finest garments."

"That is kind of you to say. I will share your compliments with her," he says. "Well, they look in good condition to me." Lebis stands up from the last wheel. Another silence suffocates me.

"I will tell my parents you stopped by and that the carriage is in fine condition," I say, breaking the silence that seemed eternal. "Thank you for stopping by," I say and turn toward the house.

"Eramane," he says, "since we are no longer complete strangers, what would you say about going to the river with me tomorrow? We could have a picnic or walk along the river's edge—or whatever you like." His words come out plainly enough, but it looks like he is going to rub a hole in the palm of his hands. At least I am not the only one who is nervous.

"I will be at my brother's home tomorrow. Mira and I have plans to ..."

"Break them," Lebis says.

"I cannot just break plans with Mira."

"Samiah has only been home a few days. I am sure that he and Mira will benefit from more time alone." I know that Lebis is right. I also note that he will not be taking no for an answer.

"Well, Lebis, maybe you should come tomorrow and ask my brother first; if he does not remove your head, I will go."

Lebis wears a brazen look. "When should I arrive?" is all he says in rebuttal.

I pause for a moment, and then it occurs to me. "Was Samiah with my mother when she requested your services?"

"Yes, he and Mira accompanied her." Lebis's confidence swells. "Samiah did threaten to remove my head, so it is important that I do not 'dishonor her in any way. She is my sister and ...'" He repeats Samiah's speech and almost pulls off a decent impression of my brother.

"Is everyone in on this?" I am angered that even my brother has taken part in this meddling. Samiah is supposed to be on my side, and now I find that he is in on this scheme. However, it is worthy to note Samiah's approval. Honestly, I do not know why I keep opposing the idea. I like Lebis, and I remember how I felt earlier when I saw Lily with him. "My family is trying to get rid of me," I say half agitated, half giggling. "Yes, I will picnic with you at the river tomorrow afternoon."

"It is settled," Lebis says in an unmistakable tone of satisfaction. He turns and jumps up on his horse. "Tomorrow, then." He nods his head and rides off into the night.

I am disturbed from my dreams when Samiah comes home in the middle of the night. I know that he must have had a great night because he came to the wrong house, and he is singing and mumbling a made-up song about his darling Mira. "Lovely, lovely, that is she! Beautiful legs … all for me!" He knocks over a vase on the table and finds it amusing that it shatters as it strikes the wooden floor. I get out of my warm bed and make my way to the hall to help him. I try to be careful of the broken glass, but it is dark; my left foot finds a large piece anyway.

"Ouch!" I exclaim. "Samiah, you drunken ogre, my foot is bleeding now!" I yell as I hobble into the kitchen for a cloth.

"I am sooo sorry, Eramane. Let me help you," he says in a drunken slur. He trips and falls to the floor.

"Are you trying to make me hate you, Samiah?" I ask, sitting to take a look at my foot. The cut is in the middle of my arch, wide and deep. I temporarily wrap it with a drying towel for dishes.

Samiah lifts his heavy head. "I am your mother," he slurs. Then sadly, as if he were about to weep, he asks, "You hate me? Why?" I shake my head at him. I want to laugh, but my foot is throbbing; it quickly takes the humor out of the situation. Our parents have been disturbed by the commotion, and now they are tiptoeing around broken glass.

"Randall, fetch me the sweeper, please," Mother asks, not moving through the broken glass any farther.

"I am your mother," I mock him quietly, managing a laugh anyway. Mother sweeps up the glass, and Father and I help Samiah to the nearest bed. I grab a blanket from the linen chest and cover him. "See you in the morning … *son*," I say, hobbling to the kitchen to properly flush out my wound. My mother sits to help me wrap it. Father went outside to stable Samiah's horse.

"Lebis stopped in to check the carriage wheels." I squint at my mother a little.

"That is wonderful. How are the wheels?" she asks, knowing that they are perfectly fine.

"They all need to be replaced," I try to say seriously, but I cannot contain my laughter. The wrap is drenched with blood and surprises my mother once she uncovers the cut.

"Eramane, this is a bad cut. We are going to have to stitch it." I cringe.

"Do not say that, Mother. Are you sure?" I loathe the idea.

"Yes, dear. I am sorry, but I must." She rises and goes to fetch proper equipment for the task.

I sit back and grip the sides of the chair. This is going to be painful. My mother douses the wound with something that smells strongly and burns so horribly that I almost cry. I clench my teeth through the entire process, and when it is finally done, my jaws hurt. "There you go, my darling," she says, tying up the end of a clean strip of cloth.

"So?" Mother returns to our conversation concerning Lebis's visit.

"So, we are going to the river tomorrow afternoon."

"Oh, that is fantastic, Eramane!"

"Mother, do not be so enthusiastic. It is only our first meeting. He has not asked me to marry him." I am slightly annoyed by her excitement.

"I am just so happy that you are actually spending time with such a nice boy. Your father and I think the world of him." Her tone changes and she becomes more serious. "You know that your father and I have turned down more than a few suitors for you. Some of them you have no knowledge of, because I simply could not bear telling you that such rascals thought they deserved you. Honestly, it would have been a waste of breath. But, Eramane, you must know that Lebis is different from most of the other suitors around here. He is a charming young man, and he is taken by you. A man like that will honor you; he will protect you; he will die for you. Do you understand, child?"

She is right. Lebis is unlike other suitors that have asked for my hand. And now that I think about it, he has put off every girl that has made an advance for his affections. He was waiting for me.

"I know, Mother. He is a special fellow."

"And he is handsome," she adds.

"Yes, and he is handsome," I agree, and for the first time I see that my mother was not meddling at all; she was cleverly bringing together two people who were fated for each other, two people who could sustain a happy and loving life together. We are interrupted by my father. He enters and walks over to the wash basin, dipping his hands into the water.

"Just as I expected, Samiah's horse was standing next to the porch, reins hanging straight down to the ground." His subtle chuckle cannot hide the fact that he is tired and mildly annoyed that he was wakened in the middle of the night to stable a horse.

It is almost twilight, and I have just said my good-byes to my parents. "Be safe today, Eramane," my father says from atop the carriage.

"I will, Father."

"Flush and dress your wound each day. You do not want infection to set in," my mother orders. And with a snap of the reins, the horses lunge and the carriage pulls away. I go back inside and curl up in my father's chair, and sleep comes for me again. I welcome it and hope that I can rest until midmorning without being disturbed.

CHAPTER THREE

AƒTERПOOП WITH LEBIS

THUMP! THUMP! THUMP! THUMP! THUMP! A frantic banging on the front door wakes me. Not yet moving from the chair, I look outside and see that not much time has passed since I went to sleep. The banging comes again. This time the door is answered. Oriana is already here, filling the wash basins and preparing a morning meal for Samiah and myself.

"Hello, m'lady. May I help you?" I hear her ask.

"Is my husband here?" It is Mira and she sounds worried.

"Mira!" I shout so that she can hear me. Oriana steps back and invites Mira in; she leads Mira to me.

"Eramane, is Samiah here? I left the mountaintop early last night; he stayed back. When I woke this morning, I could not find him. I came here first."

"No need to worry; he is here. He came here last night, singing about you; then he knocked over a vase, and it shattered on the floor." I look at my wrapped foot, and Mira follows my gaze.

"You cut yourself," she gasps. "Let me look at it."

"It is fine," I say. "I have to clean it again before we leave for your place."

"Well, Samiah will probably sleep for a while longer. Let me clean it for you, and then we can go pick some of those beautiful redtails. They will look lovely on my table." Mira insists and Oriana fetches a wash basin and a cloth.

Mira carefully unwraps my bandaged foot, making sure that she does not pull too fast. There is a little blood, but much less than we both expected. "Your mother did a wonderful job stitching this, Eramane." Mira's expression turns from being impressed to puzzlement. "For this wound to have needed stitches, it is healing remarkably fast," she says, motioning for me to examine it myself. I bring my foot up so that I can get a better look, and just as Mira said, it is healing quickly. I am less surprised than Mira; I have always healed quickly.

"I will just wipe the dried blood and wrap it back up. Then we can be on our way," Mira says.

The morning has been pleasant; I always enjoy Mira's company. I told her about my date with Lebis; she reacted as I expected: "Oh, Eramane, that is so exciting!" We have spent much of the early morning picking wildflowers in the field behind my family's home. Bright red blossoms cover the meadow. When we gather enough to comfortably carry, we take them back to the cottage to wrap them in damp linens so that they make the trip to Mira's.

My mother usually accompanies me on these flower-picking adventures. Our house is always adorned with freshly picked flowers. Gathering wildflowers is my favorite morning activity when the fields are in bloom, but soon they will all wither. Winter approaches and after the first frost the meadow will be barren until spring.

Mira is inside waking Samiah. We need to start making our way to their home if I am to have time for the tub. I am at the stables saddling Lady, while Linnox, the middle of the boys who help tend our farm, saddles Samiah's steed. I want to ride Lady back to the house, so I lead her out of the stable and hop on top of her, a task made only slightly more difficult by my injured foot. A gentle breeze blows through my hair and then ceases. I take a breath to inhale the freshness of the beautiful morning. I want so desperately for this day to be a wonderful memory I can hold on to. Will it be memorable? Or will I find that I am disappointed with the handsome blacksmith? I long for excitement. Samiah has such excitement in his life. He travels to many different lands, just as our father. And although Lebis works in town, he is has traveled to far-off places. My mother told me that Lebis used to travel with his father the way Samiah would travel with ours. Lebis has seen much of the world beyond the small village of Eludwid. Maybe one day he will take me to visit another land.

The wind picks up again and brings me back to the day. I have been in the fields all morning; if I do not bathe, I will end up smelling like horse food to Lebis. As I ride Lady up to the porch, I wonder how many more times I will ride her before she is too old for that. She borders fifteen and horses do not usually make it much further if you continue to push them. Mother will get a new horse soon, and Lady can spend her final years leisurely strolling along in the pasture.

After we arrive at Samiah and Mira's, I am more than ready for a bath. Mira asks for the tub to be filled, and I unpack while I wait. Their caretaker, a middle-aged woman named Brenna, brings me linens, soaps, and oils, and places them at the edge of the tub. I undress and unwrap my foot. When I reach the tub, I submerge myself, slowly and steadily, not wanting to put pressure on my foot. The water is the perfect temperature between warm and hot. The steam surrounds me, and I lie back and enjoy the silence. Placing a cloth over my face, I lean my head back on the warm stone and empty my thoughts. I welcome the silence; Samiah and Mira are at the other end of the house, so nothing will intrude on my relaxing moment. I plunge beneath the water to wet my hair, and the water fills my ears with its warmth. I stay under that water for a few moments, listening to my heartbeat, and letting my body float in the large tub. Then I hear someone speak my name; it is a deep voice, a man's voice. Startled, I sit up to see who is calling me. I wipe my face and look around the room. No one is there. I know that I am not mistaken. Someone spoke my name, and it was not Samiah; it is not his voice I heard.

A large mirror leans against the wall in front of me. I stare at my reflection for a moment, not knowing what to think. Had I been in the sun too long this morning?

"Eramane," the voice calls to me again. This time I see him, or what seems like a reflection of him. I search the room again, but no one is there until I look back into the mirror, and there he is. Our eyes meet, and at once, I have no desire to ever cease staring into his mesmerizing, amber eyes. He speaks again: "I will come for you tonight." His words settle in my head, and I become numb. It is as if I the beautiful stranger's words have hypnotized me, captured my soul, and I am, at once, willing to give myself over to this intruder.

But the spell is broken when Mira taps on the door. "Eramane, do not wrap your wound when you are finished. I want your brother to see what he did to you."

"Fine," I say, agitated by the intrusion. I finish my bath and wrap a linen robe around me. As I walk to my room, I notice that the pain has subsided, and my foot is only a little tender.

"Does it hurt?" Samiah asks, waiting for me to sit and prop my foot on the bed. He takes my foot in his hand, inspecting it. "Eramane, this does not look so bad. Why did mother stitch it?"

"Because it was much worse yesterday, Samiah, and maybe the astringent that mother used helped it along."

"I'd say. I should cut the stitches out. It looks like they can be removed," he says.

"I will do it tonight. It cannot hurt to leave them in a bit longer."

"Are you sure you are all right?" Samiah asks.

"I am fine." I try to rise from the bed, but Samiah and Mira are huddled over me as if I have just been pierced with an arrow and they are trying to decipher my last words.

"Hit me," Samiah says. "Smack me straight across the face. I deserve it."

"I am not slapping you, Samiah. It was an accident, after all."

"C'mon," he teases, turning his head to the side so I have a good target. "Right here." He taps his cheek.

"Why not leave and let me finish getting dressed? Lebis will be here any moment now."

"Suit yourself," he says. Then he leans down and kisses my head. "I am sorry, sister. Heal quickly." Samiah turns to his wife. "I will be outside tending the horses," he says, pulling the door closed behind him.

"Your foot is healing well, but it still needs to be wrapped," Mira says, putting my foot in her lap. We sat on the bed in their guest room while she tended to my injury. "You should sleep fine in here," Mira says. "We just purchased this bed, and it is stuffed full of goose feathers." She moves my leg off of her lap and stands to brush my hair.

"I can do that," I say, not wanting to feel like a burden.

"Nonsense, Eramane. I love to fix up hair. Besides, I am going to need the experience if our baby is a girl." Mira pauses, waiting for me to catch on. I do.

"You are with child?" I ask, filled with excitement.

"Yes," she says, swelling with joy. I stand and hug her.

"I have to go congratulate Samiah," I say, starting for the door.

"He does not know yet," Mira says. "I have not told him because I wanted to make absolutely sure."

"What do you mean?" I ask.

"I will have missed my second cycle in a few days. Once I make it that far along, I will know for certain; but, Eramane, I feel it already." Her eyes glisten with tears.

"You are pregnant, Mira. Oh, I am so happy for you both!" We hug again and then she pushes me back.

"Now, let us get your hair done before Lebis arrives." Mira pulls my hair back and braids it all the way down to my waistline, tying it with sand-colored ribbon. Then she places the bird-wing hairpin just above my ear. "All that is left is to put on your yellow dress. I will be in the kitchen," Mira says.

Lebis will be here soon, but my beautiful yellow dress is becoming a nuisance. The length is bothersome because of my wrapped foot, and the bottom of the dress keeps tangling between my feet. But I love this dress, and I am determined to wear it. I look myself over in the mirror. The hairpin and ribbon stand out against my dark brown tresses. I lift my hand to touch the hairpin; I love it. Satisfied, I hobble out to the kitchen.

"There is no way that Lebis could take another after looking at you." The wonderful compliment comes from Samiah as he rises from his chair at the kitchen table. "You know, I will have my men keeping an eye on the two of you," he says with a smirk.

"Will they hold my hand too?" I ask.

"If I tell them to, they will," he says, and they would too. We trade smiles and I pull up a seat.

"Where is Mira?" I ask.

"She said she needed to lie down for a bit. She is not feeling well." Samiah looks concerned.

"I am sure she will be fine," I say, trying to lift Samiah's concern. "She may have eaten something from the festival that has disagreed with her. You know, I was feeling unlike myself last night, but I am better now."

"You are probably right," he says. I think I convinced him. My story was not completely dishonest; I did feel unlike myself last night, right after I stepped on that shard of glass.

I hear the slowing trot of a horse just outside. Samiah looks out the kitchen window.

"Your knight has just arrived," he says. "Take that." Samiah points to a small dagger lying on the cutting block. "Keep it tied to your leg." He hands me a leather strap.

"Why would I need this?" I ask, almost worried.

"I like Lebis, I really do. But when it comes to you, I do not trust any man."

"Are you serious, Samiah? I am nervous enough without you frightening me. I am not taking it. Have your men follow us. I do not care, but I am not tying a blade to my leg." I toss the strap next to the blade.

"Take it, Eramane. I will not take no for an answer. There is nothing wrong with having help if you need it."

Samiah begins to walk to the door. "What are you doing?" I ask.

"I am just going to say hello, Eramane. He makes my weapons; it would be rude if I did not." He opens the front door halfway and, looking back to me, he says, "Put that on." He looks down at the blade, and then out of the house he goes.

"I am not wearing that." I pick up the blade and the leather strap, open a cupboard door and toss them in. I will deal with Samiah later, but not now. He will not find out until we are out of sight. I begin to close the cupboard door when I see Mira in the doorway.

"Mira!" Her presence startles me, and I shut the cupboard door less delicately than I would have liked. "Are you feeling better?"

"A bit," she says, reaching for the water pitcher. I pull a chair out for her to sit.   "I suggested to Samiah that you may have eaten something spoiled. He seemed to believe it, so you may be able to disguise your nausea for a few more days without suspicion."

"That is clever, Eramane." Her voice is dry.

"Did you vomit?" I ask.

"Quite a bit, actually." She wipes her brow. "Till there was nothing left."

"You should go back to bed and rest. It is hot, and heat never helps nausea."

"I will. I just wanted to see you off. Did Samiah ask you to wear that ridiculous blade?"

I look to the cupboard. "Yes." Mira follows my gaze.

"But you tossed it in my cabinet instead?" Mira's laugh is dry too.

"Please, Mira, do not tell him."

"Your secret is safe with me, Eramane. Now get out of here before Lebis hops back on that horse to fetch Lily."

"You are hopeless, Mira." I kiss her good-bye on the cheek. "Go back to bed."

"Have fun. Be safe," she says. I walk to the front door, take a deep breath, and open it, greeting Lebis with a friendly smile.

He is standing with his arms folded; he looks different. I am accustomed to seeing him in dark leather garments pierced with burn holes, in gloves and big boots. Like this, though, he looks bright, dressed in a light linen shirt and dark trousers. His light brown, curly hair falls just past his neck. Lebis does not look like the rugged local blacksmith any longer. I try to look him over once more before being noticed, but my chance to take him in has passed.

"Eramane," Lebis greets me with a gentleman's bow.

"Hello," I say, taking my time down the steps, favoring my injury.

"What happened?" Lebis asks, offering his hand to steady me down the last few steps.

"I stepped on a shard of glass last night."

"Does it hurt?" Lebis asks.

"Only when I am awake," I say with sarcasm. Samiah remains silent, his lips tight, as if trying to keep from revealing the world's biggest mystery. Lebis makes sure I am steady before releasing his grip. Our bodies are close, and my heart begins to race. Face-to-face, we stare at each other for a moment. His bright blues eyes make me smile.   "This is for you," Lebis says, as he presents me with a cherrywolf flower he had tied to his belt. "It is not as beautiful as you, but when I saw it, I thought of you." His sincerity is heartfelt, and my nervousness is beginning to subside. Lebis is chivalrous and deserving of my attention.

"Where did you find it?" I ask.

"On my way here, just down the path there. It caught my attention, so I stopped Kelwyn and picked it."

"These are not supposed to grow around here," I say.

"A bird must have dropped a seed from a bloom it carried," Samiah explains.

Lebis lifts the flower to my head, tucking it just below my bird-wing clip. I feel I cannot catch my breath. How am I supposed to go through with this when a simple gesture pummels me with panic? *Breathe, Eramane, you must breathe.*

"Thank you," I say. That is all I can manage to say.

Samiah breaks in, "Lebis, how is the sword coming along?" he asks, stepping forward.

"Very well, my friend," Lebis says. "Most of my recent work has been directed to travelers. But I was able to give your weapon some much-needed attention earlier this morning. A few more sessions and it will be quite a remarkable sword,"

Lebis says, his tone proud. His attention focuses back to me. "Your brother and his Riders keep me very busy. I cannot believe an unimaginable number of requests were not waiting for me this morning," Lebis says laughing. He leans in close to me and says, "They just wish they were the man standing here right now." I blush.

"Well, I will not hold the two of you any longer. Get going." Samiah puts his hands on our backs and pushes us toward Lebis's horse. Lebis helps me up, since I should not put much weight on my foot, and turns to Samiah.

"I will be nothing less than a gentleman," he says.

"I have complete faith in that, Lebis. You are an honorable man; otherwise, I would have already run you through." Samiah's eyes widen. He was mostly serious. They shake hands again and Lebis jumps onto his tan mare, Kelwyn. Lord Danius gave Lebis this mare because of his outstanding craftsmanship. Lord Danius has not lost any of his conflicts since Lebis has been crafting their weapons. Lord Danius believes that the strength and durability of the weapons has a major role in that feat. When the enemies' swords would break off into pieces, Lebis's weapons held strong. Giving Lebis the mare as a token of gratitude made Kelwyn special to Lebis, and her bloodline makes her irreplaceable, since the line is usually only passed to nobility. Kelwyn is like Lebis's workmanship: strong, lasting, and dependable.

We ride slowly up the hill that leads to the river. Once we top the hill, I lean up to Lebis's ear. "Let her go!"

Turning his head slightly, he asks, "Are you sure?"

"Yes!" I confirm.

"She is really fast," he shouts proudly.

"Yes! Yes! I am sure! Let her go!" My excitement reassures him, and he gives his beautiful horse the command. Kelwyn does not hesitate. She lunges and we gallop down the hillside into the meadow. The mare runs so fast that the wind whistles as it passes my ears. The flowers part as we trample through them. Insects fly in all directions to avoid our sudden and unstoppable intrusion. The moment engulfs me, and I let go of Lebis to put my hands out. I lift my head to the sky and inhale all of the smells from the earth. I feel the sun trying to kiss my skin, but it cannot keep up with us. I squeeze Kelwyn tightly with my legs; her slender physique enables me to hold on tight. I wish that this moment of freedom will last forever.

My moment of enjoyment is short-lived, as the image of the beautiful man I saw earlier revisits me. But I decide immediately that I want to dwell on this moment, my moment with Lebis, his magnificent mare, and the beautiful meadow. I open my eyes and in an instant the image is gone, replaced by my beautiful surroundings. I lean forward and put my arms around Lebis's waist, gently latching on to him. He looks back to me, and I see a smile come over him before he can turn away.

"There it is!" Lebis shouts. "Just beyond the tree line!" Kelwyn slows her run to a trot, then to a walk. "We will have to walk her in. She gets a little spooked by the shadows. Once we are in, she will be all right," Lebis says, pulling back on her reins. He dismounts, drops the reins, and offers his hand to me. I slide down the side of the horse and land on the softest, greenest grass I have ever seen. As I look around, I realize that I have never been to this part of the river before. Usually my family goes to the waterfall by the cliffs. Here, though, the river runs through the forest, very secluded and peaceful.

We walk into the woods. Lebis searches for a spot to lay down our picnic blanket. He locates a brilliant green, moss-covered patch right next to the edge of the river. The forest is thick, but beams of light shoot through in every place they can, giving it a dreamlike quality: a setting fit for fairy tales. The beauty of this place is astounding. Lebis throws out a thick, red, velvet blanket, stirring the woodland creatures. Blue and yellow butterflies flutter all around, and their wings twinkle when they catch beams of sunlight piecing through the trees. A rabbit hops along the edge of the river, and little birds migrate from tree to tree, trying to get a closer look at the humans who have invaded their homes. The mare, on her own accord, saunters over to the river's edge and lowers her head to the water, sucking in its cold refreshment. I am curious to know how cold the water feels. I edge up slowly and kneel down to submerge my fingertips.

I put my hands in the clear water; it is cold, and it sends me back to when my father took Samiah and me to the river. I ran from my brother, knowing he wanted to toss me in the water. He eventually caught me and threw me into the river, jumping in himself right after. The water was cold and took our breath away. The day had been unseasonably hot, so after a few seconds we adjusted to the water and enjoyed our swim.

The water is clear, and I can see all the way to the bottom. In some parts the sun reaches the bottom and makes the riverbed pebbles sparkle. While I am taking in the beauty of the forest, I am suddenly jolted as I recall the words from the beautiful stranger: "I will come for you tonight." I drop my view of the canopy down to the river water. As I peer into the water, watching a leaf slowly float by, I see *his* reflection again. It is blurry at first and then forms clearly. I stare at him and he stares back at me. *Tonight, Eramane.* I am hearing him in my thoughts! I continue to stare into the water, hypnotized by the image, just as I was earlier. His words penetrate my skin, and I feel as if I have been stung by thousands of little bees.

I cannot move my eyes away from his, and I feel as if I am being pulled closer to the water's surface, as if something below the water is pulling me in. At first I struggle with the sensation; then an eagerness to give in comes over me, and I let it take me closer to the water's surface.

"Dinner is served." Lebis's words break the spell, and I quickly recover from the trance. I splash at the water, and the reflection blurs and is gone just as quickly as it appeared. I stand, eager to feel in control of myself, when I feel Lebis put his arms around me. I feel his breath on the back of my neck. "Are you thinking of going for a swim?" Lebis asks as I turn to face him.

"No, the water is freezing. *You* can go for a swim. I will hold your clothes." I hold my arms out.

"And run off with them, leaving me in the water to freeze,"

"No. You can get out and fetch them from me," I tease. His eyes are bright and when he turns his head just the right way, the sun rays light them up, making them twinkle like the butterfly wings. I am no longer nervous in his company. A soothing calm washes through me, and for the first time I see, in Lebis's twinkling eyes, that he would rather be nowhere else than with me.

Our hands touch; he pulls me close to him. "You are so beautiful," he says, and he kisses my forehead. He holds his hand out, and I take it. We both walk, hands locked, to the red picnic blanket.

A loaf of honey bread, a cut of cheese, and a bowl of berries are laid out in the middle of the blanket.

"So, I brought all of this. What did you bring?" he asks, looking to me for an immediate reply.

"Seriously?" I ask. "I brought nothing. I would have; I just assumed that …"

"It is fine, Eramane. I was only joking." He has a deep gut chuckle. I sigh and shake my head. We pick at the food Lebis brought. The bread is warm, the cheese is soft, and the berries are a sweet I have not had in quite some time. They are mouthwatering, almost too good. As I tear another piece of bread from the loaf, I feel it proper to compliment Lebis. He has put together a fine picnic.

"This is lovely, Lebis, really. And these?" I motion to the berries. "Did your father grow them? First the cherrywolf flower, now the berries. You are full of surprises."

"Yes, my father grew them, and thank you," he says. "*You* are lovely."

CHAPTER FOUR

Adikiah at the River

WE HAVE HAD OUR FILL of bread and cheese; I watch as Lebis tosses the last of the food to curious forest creatures, the ones brave enough to approach us. None of the animals got to taste the berries; we ate all of those. We spend the rest of the afternoon trading stories of our childhoods. Lebis tells me of how he has worked farmlands and metals since he was a boy. His parents are happily married, and Lebis's father works their lands, which produce much of Eludwid's fruits. My father wanted to grow fruit crops, but the soil on our farmland is more suitable for wheat. My family and others like mine, with the wheat soil, buy our fruits from the market in the middle of town.

Lebis's father is an entrepreneur. He travels to collect seeds from other lands and brings them home to grow and sell to the townspeople. He has a gift that produces wonderfully delicious fruits, like the berries we had for lunch. Lebis, on the other hand, does not have such a talent; instead he has the knack for bending steel. Lebis studied this trade from Whiney but far exceeded the old man's skills. "I taught myself the rest," he says proudly.

My laughter fills the woods as Lebis finishes telling me a story of a wild skunk that intruded on his eleventh birth celebration. The skunk sprayed inside of his home, and everyone had to leave because of the putrid smell. For days Lebis smelled like skunk, and so did his friends. Lebis added that he found that same skunk a few days later and decided that he should not kill the little creature. Instead he brought it home and asked his parents if he could keep it. His parents were in shock that the skunk had not yet sprayed, and they quickly ordered Lebis to return the skunk to its home in the forest. Lebis did as he was told. "But I visited that skunk every day for the rest of the summer, until one day I went and it was not there," Lebis finishes. The woodland creatures do not respond to the laughter; it is getting late and they have already nestled themselves in for the night. Kelwyn snorts as if she thinks Lebis has forgotten about her.

"She should be a concern of yours; she is the only woman in my life." He is grinning, but I am momentarily bewildered.

"Kelwyn?" I ask. Lebis looks past me. I turn to follow his stare. "Well she *is* lovely, and I am sure that she will not complain about you tracking your filthy boots through the stables," I say, smirking.

I am sitting close to him, and we are sharing a wool wrap to keep us warm from the chilly late-evening air. Lebis and I stare at each other. My skin begins to tickle; I know what is supposed to happen next: a kiss. The forest is so quiet that I believe Lebis can hear my heart pounding. He leans in close, our noses almost touching, and speaks to me softly.

"I have waited so long to be in this moment," he says, his eyes gleaming with pride and appreciation. I say nothing, just smile anxiously. "You are the most beautiful woman I have ever seen, Eramane." He tilts his head a little. "You take my breath away." His words are flattering, and I do not have the desire to turn away. Just before our lips meet, Lebis's appearance is replaced with the image of the beautiful stranger. I pull away.

"I am sorry, Eramane. I should not have assumed …" Lebis is afraid that he has insulted me.

"No, it is not you. I just thought that I saw something," I explain.

"What was it? What did you see?"

"I am not sure," I say. "It was nothing of importance." I dismiss the hallucination and once again give Lebis my full attention. Both of us are unnerved now, and what would have been the perfect moment for a kiss passes. But Lebis derives an opportunity for a kiss when he gently strokes my neck with his fingertips. I breathe him in, adoring his scent with every breath, and if we never meet again, I will always remember his smell. I cannot push aside thoughts of regret, sorry that it is only now that we have truly discovered each other. I so long to become acquainted with this remarkable man and I can almost hear my mother in my head saying, *See? I told you!*

He slips my dress strap down and kisses my shoulder. "I want to be with you and you with me, Eramane—always. Does your heart feel the same?" he asks.

"Yes, you are what I want," I admit.

"Good, then … I have secured a second chance to be with you." Without hesitation, he replaces my dress strap and jumps up, standing above me with his arms stretched down toward me. "Come on, I need to get you back home before your brother comes looking for us," he says, pulling me up to stand. "I could use some assistance," he says, looking around at the picnic items. I am still a little unraveled from his soft kiss, but I gather my senses and dust pieces of lint from the wool wrap off my dress.

"It is darker now than I would like for it to be, and the forest can be a dangerous place at night. We should get going," he says and tosses his belongings over his shoulder, turning to look for Kelwyn. "She has wandered off," he says. Lebis sends out a sharp whistle in an attempt to summon his mare. He walks a few yards away from me, scanning the barely lit forest. I keep my eyes on him and even begin to follow, but my injured foot finds a rock that sends an agonizingly sharp pain up my leg. I immediately stop following Lebis, but he has not noticed yet, and in an instant I am alone. Lebis is not far from me, but the forest has us separated by its shadows, making it seems as if we are miles apart.

I try to keep my focus in the direction I last saw Lebis. The moon is full and pokes through in places, but with night set in, I begin to feel panic rise. There is a story told to young girls, for the purpose of keeping them safe, of a maiden being lost in a dark forest; it does not end well, and it is all I can think about, being out here alone. "Lebis!" I hear no reply. "Lebis, where are you?" Again, nothing, and I have moved from panic to true fear. The forest seems to spin around me; I am dizzy and cannot get a sense of direction. I lean on a tree and close my eyes. Open, close, open, close, open—the forest slows down, and when the fuzzy image of spinning trees comes into focus, so does he.

Looking straight forward into the darkness, the stranger appears, slowly walking toward me. I am not afraid, because his appearance is curious to me, not harmful. But as he gets closer, his beautiful amber eyes change to a fiery orange color; they are fixed on me, peering beyond me, it feels. "Eramane, I have come to take you with me." Now I am frightened.

"Eramane!" Lebis finds his way back to me. "I was worried about you. I thought you were following, and when I turned back, you were gone."

"It is my foot. I stepped on a rock. But, Lebis, we have to go now." Lebis sees that I am upset beyond just being left alone.

"What happened? Are you all right?"

"Lebis, something is out here." I explain to him that I saw a man in the forest. He scans the forest in all directions and takes my hand. "Can you walk?"

"Yes."

"All right, this way." He leads me through the darkness; the trees usher us along, causing us to turn this way and that. A noise ahead stops us in our tracks. We listen more closely. "It is Kelwyn," Lebis says, and darts the direction of the sound.

Lebis and I are shaken when a powerful gust of wind passes between us and up into the trees. We follow it with our eyes. I look to Lebis. "What was that?" I ask.

"I do not know," he says and takes hold of my hand again. "We must hurry. I have a sword on Kelwyn." We run a few more paces. "Kelwyn!" Lebis gasps. He reaches his mare before I do. He turns and grabs me, covering my eyes. I can smell raw meat; the stench of exposed animal bowels fills my nostrils. I rip his hand away from my eyes and see the carnage that is Kelwyn's fate. I scream and Lebis grabs my face to get my attention.

"Whoever did this is probably still here. I know this is an awful thing, but we have to get out of these woods and into the open. We must hurry." He searches the ground for his sword. He locates the sheath only a few inches away from Kelwyn's head. Lebis snatches it up; he takes my hand and we run.

We dart through the trees, and soon the forest spews us into the meadow. I am frightened and devastated by the image of Kelwyn that forever will be burned in my memory. *Who would do that to her?*

I feel the powerful gust of wind again. Nothing in the wild is moving, but we have our own windstorm circling us. "Lebis, what is happening?" I cry as the cyclone forces us together.

He holds on to me tightly. "I will not let anything happen to you, Eramane, I promise!" he shouts. The wind is deafening, and as easily as it brought us together, it moves between us and forces us to separate. Lebis is aggressively thrown away from me. He stumbles to catch his balance. The whirlwind travels up into the trees of the forest once more. We stare at each other in astonishment. "We have to put distance between us and the forest," Lebis orders. Again we run, but my wound has reopened, and I am bleeding and in pain. I try to run despite it, but where are we running to? There is nothing around for at least a mile.

The sound of the rushing wind comes again, only this time it has a form. An enormous creature flies down from the heavens and lands inches away from me. Its glowing, fire-colored eyes fixate on me and burn through to my core. The night is so dark that all I can see are its eyes, and I know, at that moment, that the beast means to kill Lebis. I realize instantly that Lebis is no match for this frightful *thing*, and my companion will die trying to defend me. I look across to Lebis and see that he knows this too.

The beast searches my face with its burning eyes. I am terrified by its presence, and the intensity behind its eyes forces me to close mine, unable to bear the gaze from the beast any longer. I hear it move and I open my eyes to see it advance toward Lebis. The creature moves with impressive speed and is able to quickly and effortlessly disarm Lebis with one strike from its massive hand.

Lebis is knocked to the ground by this attack and loses his sword. He looks around for it with no success. The creature stands in front of Lebis, towering over him. Lebis scrambles to his feet in an effort to defend against the next attack. The

beast stretches out its wings, flexing. It steps aside and exposes
Lebis's sword. Lebis looks down at the sword. Laughing, the
beast orders Lebis to engage. "Take it," the beast's deep, commanding voice vibrates in my chest. It takes another step
away from the sword, giving Lebis more room to snatch up
his weapon. He grips his sword tight, his knuckles white, and
aims it at the creature.

"Who sent you? A summoner? A caster?"

"I am summoned by no one, cast by no one." The beast
rolls its shoulders forward. "Are you going to use that?" it
taunts Lebis.

"I will if I have to." Lebis stands guarded. "What is your
purpose in all of this? We are no challenge for you."

"That is right; you are no challenge for me, yet there you
stand with your sword, ready. What do you think you can do
with that?"

"What do you want?" Lebis shouts. The beast turns from
Lebis and looks at me.

"Her," it says. And while it focuses on me, Lebis lunges
and slices the beast across its leg. It snarls and faces its attacker.

"You will have to kill me first," Lebis says.

"I know," the beast says and jumps at Lebis, taking hold of
him effortlessly. With one of its hands around Lebis's throat,
the beast grabs his face with the other and separates Lebis from
his essence.

"*No!*" I scream. Lebis's body is cast down, landing at my
feet. I collapse to him, take his head in my arms, and search
for any sign of life. I know I will not find it; the beast has

what is left of Lebis. "Oh no! Lebis!" I cry out. I rest my head on his, my tears dripping on his face. I feel I am about to be consumed with grief, and then anger emerges, replacing my sadness. My abhorrence is indescribable, immeasurable, and undeniable. I stand and scream, to the beast, to the meadow, the forest, the world. "Let him go!" I demand. The beast looks at me, surprised. It releases Lebis's essence, what faintly remains of it, anyway. The creature seems to have absorbed some of it already. That is what it looked like, as if it were soaking Lebis in through its hand somehow. The remainder breaks apart and fades into nothing, but I am not satisfied. I want to scream so loudly that my noise causes the beast to break apart and fade into nothing too, and picturing this fuels my pitch, so I continue to scream.

The ground begins to tremble; I have the beast's attention. It looks down at the earth and watches as cracks ripple through the ground. The beast looks at me and back to the ground again. I scream so violently that my voice begins to break. My voice is hoarse, but I will not stop until the earth cracks open and engulfs the horrible beast.

The creature leaps in my direction and lands in front of me; I look up at the massive creature towering over me, and it is like being at the bottom of a mountain and looking up toward its peak. "Eovettzi˜ nomistara," the beast's words lull me; I want to run, but my body is numb and my mind calms. The ground begins to settle, an action that gives relief to the beast.

"We belong to each other now," the beast declares as it grabs my limp body and takes me up into the darkness.

CHAPTER FIVE

Mountain Palace

CRACKLING FLAMES FROM THE OVERSIZED hearth touch my face with their heat and wake me from my void. I feel as though I have been asleep for days, without having dreams or any other reassurance of existence. I am lying on a white fur on the floor of a chamber. The bright fur stuns my vision momentarily; I have had my eyes closed for too long. I move my fingers through the fur; it is soft and smells like wood and smoke. Where am I? I blink my eyes to adjust my vision, and it begins to clear. Then my mind clears. *Lebis!* I sit up, and fright surges through me. My eyes search the room for my abductor. Where is it? It is dark in the corners of the chamber; does it lurk there? The chamber is a large stone room with no outside openings, and the ceiling is so high that I cannot see where it ends. I rise from the soft fur bedding and put my feet onto the cold floor. It is not until I stand on the chamber floor that I notice my foot has been re-bandaged. I look around the room, desperately trying to see into the darkness. If that *thing* is in here with me, I would rather discover it now than wait in wonder of my fate. I make my way to the shadowed corners. I see nothing, for now I am alone.

The rock walls have pieces of crystal that catch the reflection from the fire, causing them to twinkle like the night sky. I feel as if I am atop a mountain, surrounded only by the starlit skies. I walk slowly toward one of the walls, touching one of the sparkling crystals. The warmth of the large fire does not reach the walls, so I go back to it for comfort. I stand in front of the hearth feeling the flame's heat begin to lightly toast my skin. I stare into the flames, and their color reminds me of what brought me here, those fire-colored eyes! Images of Lebis flash inside of the flames, like a reflection in a mirror replaying that horrible event. Tears fill my eyes and blur the flames. I lie down on the white fur again and weep until I lose myself again to the bliss of sleep.

My breath is taken by a swift, musky draft. I am aware that I am still in the room with the twinkling walls and golden fire pit, but when I wake this time I can sense the presence of someone else in the chamber. However, my eyes cannot find anyone. I had hoped that death would find me in my slumber; instead it passed me over, left me alive, in the captivity of a monster. I am at the mercy of the beast that murdered Lebis, robbed me of an innocent life, and confiscated my future. Only where is this murderer? I do not believe that I can bear to gaze upon that creature again. The horrid memories spin through my head, and I wonder if I will go mad harboring all of them.

Creak, the door to my chamber opens. Hinges squeak and rattle, taking me away from my thoughts. I am suddenly keenly aware of my vulnerability, not having the safety of a closed door. "Come, Eramane," a raspy, cracking voice says. I stand and listen for the voice to speak again. "Do not be afraid; you are safe here," it says. My eyes dart around intently, not finding the source of these words.

"What do you want from me? Why have you brought me here?" I shout. My voice carries around the chamber, echoing off the stone. The door closes, leaving me alone once more, alone with my thoughts.

I do not know how long I have been held captive—hours, days? It could be either, for I have battled exhaustion the entire time, sleeping most of it. I am certain that my brother is searching for me by now. I imagine him and his Riders invading this stone prison and saving me. I have dreamt that scenario several times. It is a hope that keeps me from walking into the fire that continuously burns, hot and strong. My daydream of rescue is intruded on as the creaking of hinges and jarring of metal accompany the opening of my chamber door. There is no dark, odorous cloud this time. Again a voice, seeming to radiate from the walls themselves, offers a meal to me. Taking the offer as a cue, my stomach rumbles and gnaws at me, as if trying to claw its way out, hoping to find food on its own, in the belief that I have given up on its need of sustenance. I am starving but afraid to leave the chamber. I stare at the open door, wondering what fate awaits me if I walk through it. The door begins to close, but this time my fear of the unknown is second to my need of nourishment. "Wait, please," I say, choking back my words, afraid to actually say them. The door pauses. I walk toward it, and it waits for me.

I cannot see anything outside of the door, but I am compelled to continue through the opening anyway. I look to my right, into the darkness, and there is nothing. I look left, and it offers the same. My body is numb with fear, but I cannot seem to control its will to find food. My body moves me forward while my mind pleads for me to turn around and run back to the warm fur next to the hearth; it is desperately trying to fight against going into the dark hallway

As I proceed down the dark corridor, torches hanging from the walls begin to ignite with my every step. The walkway appears to be endless, yet with each grumble from my belly, I am compelled to proceed. I turn to look behind me; there is nothing there, not even the torches that burned a moment ago. Complete darkness backs me. All I can navigate is the way in front of me. I follow the torches until I come to another door, an oversized, wooden double door, with black iron rings the size of wagon wheels hanging from the center. The doors are so big that it seems like I will need a team of plow horses to open them. I stand in front of the wooden barriers and watch with intense curiosity as they slowly open on their own. Finally, the enormous doors cease to move, and my eyes take in a beautiful sight.

Candles upon candles illuminate this great room. They line the entire wall that is directly in front of me. Various heights and shapes of candles sit on stones that poke out of the wall. Some have long drips of wax hanging down, almost touching the floor. Others look as though they were just lit.

To my left a hearth harnesses an army of flames. I feel the burn of the fire on my skin. I stand there a moment, closing my eyes, to take in the power of the roaring flames. The walls surrounding the fire are shiny and black, like onyx. On each side of the fireplace stand glowing amber pillars, illuminated by the raging fire. Each of these pillars runs from the chamber floor to the ceiling. I never could have imagined a fireplace being so beautiful.

An iron chandelier the size of a horse carriage hangs from thick black chains above the center of a long table. Its design is intricate and looks as though it took many years to craft. There is no wall to my right; it is completely open to the night sky, where the big, round, blue moon imposes its radiant presence on the chamber. I gaze at the moon; it seems close enough for me to touch were I to lean out of the opening. It is so intrusive that I believe, for a moment, that if I jump from the ledge, I might land on the surface of that luminous globe. The immaculate beauty of the place arouses me, and I feel exhilarated.

"Have you ever seen anything like this?" a deep, soothing voice asks from behind me. Turning, my body tenses, and then my eyes look on the face of the voice, the stranger with the beautiful amber eyes. I look up at him; he is much taller than I. Never have I seen a human so beautiful; he is intimidating, with hair as black as a starless night draping down to his mid-back. His eyes remind me of nothing other than the amber columns next to the hearth in this chamber; they glow brilliantly against his golden skin. He wears a black garment that wraps around his waist and stretches down to the floor. And although he has a youthful appearance, his mannerisms and the way he speaks reveal wisdom that can be gained only from the experience of living a long life

"This is the most glorious place I have ever seen," I say, looking away from his piercing eyes. But then I lock back on them. "How did I get here? Where is that ... "

He interrupts. "You are safe here. This is my home." My questions are so numerous that I cannot seem to form them individually. I take a deep breath.

"And the voice in the chamber?" I ask.

"That was one of my servants; they like to stay in the shadows."

"If you did not want me to be afraid, why did you not fetch me yourself?"

"It is not wise to approach a fearful animal, Eramane. I wanted you to come out on your own."

I take in what he says, analyzing his explanation. And despite all that he has offered, he has yet to explain why and how he visited me at Samiah's and the river. I listen to his words in my head, trying to make sense of it all. He must be a summoner or a type of caster, or both. With this conclusion, I again find myself fearful. I cannot speak to him, afraid of his ability to inflict whatever harm he wishes. I try to hold my tears, but they have filled my eyes, and I can no longer keep them at bay. He sees this and breaks my thoughts.

"You are still afraid," he says.

"Why should I not be? You are a practitioner of the craft. You told me you were coming for me. And you expect me to feel safe? Who are you!" I blurt out swift and sharp. I could bite my tongue off. My lips tighten as I regret having opened them.

"I am Adikiah, and this is my home, my mountain," he says. "But what good is all of this," he gestures to the extravagant room, "if my eyes are the only ones to behold it?" He sees that I am unsatisfied with his answer. "I know of your loneliness, of desire for more than what is allowed for a young woman. I noticed you walking through the streets of your village during its festival, the empty look on your face. No one there can give you what I can, Eramane," he finishes.

I am not sure if this is real, for it feels like a dream. When am I going to wake?

"This is not a dream for you to wake from in the morning," he says.

"You can read my thoughts?" I ask, frightened and offended.

"No, I cannot read your thoughts, though your face I can." He offers his hand. "Come, a meal awaits you. We have much to discuss later, but first let us eat." I hesitate only a moment, for my hungry belly will not wait any longer.

We sit at the long table in the room of candles and moonlight, and I watch in silence as something inhumanly human enters the chamber. It is tall and thin. Even underneath a thick black cloak, I can make out its emaciated features. Softly uttered words from Adikiah's lips send the cloaked being out of the chamber, but in moments several more return with plates of food. I assume them to be his servants. I reflexively lean away, as one of the servants places a plate in front of me. I get a good look at this one. It is tall and thin, just like the first one I saw. It may in fact be the first one; I cannot tell. The face of this servant is masked by dark shadows cast by its cloaks, as if it has no face at all. The servant has long, skinny fingers, the color of a dull gray stone, with long, ragged fingernails that taper into points. I do not study the servant for very long before the smell of my meal reaches my nostrils. I turn my focus to the plate and forget about everything else; I just want to eat.

I am eating meats from animals I have never tasted before, and I cannot remember ever being as hungry as I am at this moment. I tear at the food, as if I am eating for the first time. The shadowlike servants scurry about, replenishing our plates with every bite. Adikiah makes only small gestures, and they grant his every command. These tall figures unsettle me; they are not human. I look across to Adikiah.

"They frighten you," he says, looking at the servant next to me.

"Yes, a little … they are not human." I strain not to offend them, but the longer they linger, the more uneasy I become.

"No, they are not human. They are mere remnants of their previous form," he states, as if his explanation is a cure-all to my rising fear. My eyes keep careful watch on the servant clos-est to me. Adikiah notices my discomfort and orders the ser-vants away.

"They are my servants, Eramane. Their only purpose is to do as I command. Do not fear them. I would torture them infinitely if they even thought about harming you." His words relieve some of my apprehension, momentarily at least. I look down at my food and begin again to eat pieces of everything. The meats, the breads, the colorful vegetables, they all melt in my mouth. I sip on a glass of sweet water infused by fruits and, for a moment, lose myself in the satisfaction of filling my belly. Adikiah sits at the opposite end of the table, eating at a pace much slower than mine. Mostly he is focused on me, as if he is studying my movements.

The frequency of the sharp clank from my fork hitting the plate slows and soon ceases entirely; I am full. "Are you finished with your meal?" he asks.

"Yes," I reply. Adikiah stands from the table and walks over to me.

"Come with me. I want to show you something," he says, holding out his hand. I look up at him and realize that there is really no choice in the matter, and besides, he did order my belly to be filled. If he had ill intentions for me, would not it have been easier to let me starve to death in the twinkling chamber?

We walk down the corridor that leads to the chamber where I awoke. I know that the chamber is not where we are headed only as we pass it. A few torches are lit down the entire length of the corridor. It does not seem to be endless, as it did before, when only a few torches lit my way. Yet even with the torches lit, this place is dark. I stay close to Adikiah, afraid that if I do not, I might be taken by the shadows. Ahead I see another large door. Adikiah makes a quick gesture with his hand, and the doors part. We get closer and I catch the smallest movement: the bottom of a cloak. I did not see it before;

it stayed out of sight in the shadows. One of the cloaked servants opened the door, and it must have been a servant that opened my chamber door both times, and the door to the eating chamber. I am glad that I did not see the servants before, for if I had, I might have chosen to remain on the white fur.

We enter a smaller room, where only stairs occupy the space. They lead up in a circular pattern.

"This way," he ushers, and we begin to walk up the staircase. The stairs are stones that protrude from the wall, supported by nothing underneath. We walk up many stairs that take us up inside his mountain palace. Adikiah holds my hand as if not to lose me. This gesture scares me; his hand is what I distrust the most, because holding it makes me feel ... powerless.

We continue up the stairs. I watch the movements in his back as we make our way up. He is defined, powerful. We top the stairs and exit through a door that leads us out of the mountain's interior. The space is airy, and looks as though the hands of giants carved it from the rock. There are no walls, just ruggedly sculpted columns that support the overhang of rock above us. This open space is a welcoming environment compared to the darkness of the long corridors and dimly lit chambers. It is night and I cannot see beyond the columns, but I hear the sound of waves crashing on rocks below. Large black lanterns hang from the rock columns, and they flicker against what can only be an ocean breeze. This place is a spectacle, but then again, everything about Adikiah's palace is that way.

In the middle of this ocean overlook, a sleeping area is situated, similar to the one in the chamber where I woke. This area has more furs, making a larger area to lie in. It looks as if it is a nesting den for a pack of wolves. Five chiseled steps lead up to this area, encircling it. I stare at the fur throws for a few moments; Adikiah's hand is no longer a matter of my concern.

CHAPTER SIX

SAMIAH'S SEARCH

"WAKE UP, LOVE." MIRA TUGS on Samiah's foot. He jerks his leg up to get it out of Mira's reach, hitting his nose with his knee.

"Ouch!" Samiah grabs his nose. Mira bursts into laughter and bends down next to Samiah's face.

"I am sorry, my love. I only meant to wake you," she says, calming her laughter. "The sun shines and the day is warm. Let us go to the market." She rises and cinches the linen wrapping her. "I saw the most beautiful scarf yesterday. Maybe the merchant has not left town yet." Mira turns to walk out of the room. "But first I would like a bath. Would you like to join me? I had Brenna draw fresh, hot water." Her linens fall to the floor, and she slowly strides out of the room. This has Samiah's attention, and he springs from the bed, chasing her into the washroom.

They soak in the steaming water, kissing and nuzzling each other. There is a knock at the door. "Yes!" Samiah shouts.

"I beg your pardon, sir, but there is a man here for you."

"What man?" Samiah asks.

"He said his name is Inandaug." Samiah rises from the hot bath water, steam coming off his skin.

"Hold on. I am coming," he announces. "I will be right back. Do not remove yourself from this tub." He kisses his wife and drapes a robe around himself. As Samiah makes his way to the front door, he passes Eramane's room and notices that she is not there; more concerning is that her room looks exactly as it did yesterday, a green dress laid out across her bed, a dress she did not choose to wear yesterday. Samiah turns and walks back to the washroom. He pokes his head in the door. "Did you see Eramane this morning?" he asks.

"She was not in her room this morning. I assumed she went out to the stables."

"What about that dress lying on her bed? Was it not the one she left there yesterday?" Mira ponders Samiah's question and realizes what he is concluding.

"Yes, it is the same. Does this mean that she never returned yesterday evening?"

"I am not sure. Did you not notice her arrive back home before you went to bed yesterday evening?" he asks.

"I was feeling ill, Samiah; it was still daylight when I lay down for bed. What about you? Did you check on her last night when you returned from town?"

"When I came in, I saw the blade and strap that she took with her lying on the cutting block. I assumed she made it home safe."

"I took it from the cupboard, sir," a feeble voice admits. Samiah looks behind him and sees Brenna.

"You took what from the cupboard?" he asks.

"Yesterday evening while I was preparing supper, I saw the blade and strap in the dish cupboard and thought it a strange place for blades and leathers, so I placed them on the cutting block. I am sorry, sir," she says without looking at him. Samiah looks back to his wife as the situation becomes clearer to him.

"Would you mind checking the stables for me while I speak with Inandaug?"

"Of course." Mira stands and grabs her robe. Samiah rushes back to the Rider at his door, leaving wet footprints on the floors as he goes. He reaches the door and pulls it open with a jerk. Inandaug slouches, his right hand resting on the top of his sheathed sword. Everything about the way he stands, shoulders hunched forward, head low, eyes hooded by a heavy brow, has Samiah convinced this visit regards Eramane.

"High Commander," Inandaug greets Samiah.

"Inandaug, what is the matter?" Samiah asks, knowing something is terribly wrong by the tight look on his Rider's face. None of his men would bother him while he was home unless it was of dire importance. Before Inandaug can reply, Samiah interrupts, "Is it Eramane?" Inandaug's expression answers his question. "What is it?" Samiah asks as he grabs Inandaug by his arm and pulls him inside the house.

Inandaug follows Samiah to the back of the house, where he dresses. Hastily, Inandaug tells Samiah what he knows. "This morning I took my sons to the meadow near the waterfalls. We were bow hunting and we decided to ride the horses along the river to spear fish." Samiah is already putting his undergear on, and Inandaug takes a breath before finishing his words. He stares at Samiah for a moment, as if Samiah might read his mind so that he does not have to finish his sentence. Samiah looks at Inandaug with eagerness.

"What did you see, Inandaug?" Samiah asks through a clenched jaw, half not wanting to hear the answer. Samiah stands frozen for a moment; he knows he will not want to hear the news from Inandaug. Samiah gathers himself and steadily finishes gathering his belongings while Inandaug continues.

"First we saw a horse that had been relieved of its insides. Then we found a hair ribbon, so we went out to the open to see if we could find who the ribbon and the horse belonged to." Inandaug gulps another time and tries to finish his report. "We found the blacksmith that your sister was with."

"I will kill him!" Samiah rages as he attaches his knives to his belt. Grabbing his sword, Samiah darts for the door.

"He is already dead, sir," Inandaug announces. Samiah turns to face him. "We found his body in the meadow. There were no fatal wounds, only some minor cuts and bruises." Inandaug finishes and looks to Samiah for a course of action.

"Where is Eramane?" shouts Samiah.

Mira enters the room, out of breath. "She is not at the stables, Samiah. What is going on?" she asks, tears welling in her eyes.

Inandaug addresses Samiah. "We could not find her, sir. We were hoping to find her here." The Rider sadly hangs his head, as if he were to blame for Eramane's disappearance.

"Eramane! Eramane!" shouts Samiah as he searches the home, hoping that maybe the attack happened after her safe return. Although Samiah knows that Lebis would not need to pass back through the meadow to return to his own home, he holds on to the hope that Eramane was not with him. He goes to her room once more, the kitchen, and the quiet room near the back of the house that Samiah and Mira have prepared for a baby. He can find no sign of her. Samiah bolts through the back door to see if she is sitting under the large shade tree near the spring; she is not there either. "Please be in here," Samiah begs as he makes his way to recheck the stables, the last place to look for Eramane. He shouts her name repeatedly until he reaches the stable doors, giving them a hard shove open. "*Eramane!*" No reply. "Where are you!?" Samiah is overwhelmed at the thought of Eramane being dead. He rubs his head and eyes for a moment, trying to gather himself.

"She has vanished, High Commander?" Inandaug asks from behind. Samiah regains his composure and focuses on finding his sister.

"Inandaug, send a Rider to inform my parents in Dandridge that they need to return home; then meet me at the river waterfalls. I will get the Ghosts. Hurry; we have to search the area!" Samiah commands and grabs gear to saddle his horse.

At the waterfalls, Samiah gathers with Nahmas, Terrin, Aurick, Inandaug, and ten other men that he commands in Lord Danius's forces. The Ghosts cluster together, making their distinct features stand out above the other Riders. Their scalps and faces are hairless, their skin pale, and their eyes the color of the clearest blue skies. Years of practicing their craft has changed their natural appearance to resemble their ability. Their grayed leather clothing fits tightly and exactly, so that it blends when they trace cast.

Samiah dismounts and slowly makes his way to the area where the Riders found Lebis. As he moves closer, he notices the places in the grass that have been trampled down, and in other places, clumps of dirt and grass lie scattered about. This is where the conflict occurred, and Samiah wonders about the placement of Lebis's corpse.

"Why is his body all the way over here, when the conflict took place way over there?" Samiah asks aloud. He squats to Lebis's body. "What happened to you?" Samiah looks over the remains. "And what has become of my sister?" Samiah searches the body for wounds, picking up Lebis's limbs and examining them. Finding nothing more than what Inandaug already stated, Samiah lifts the head, feeling the back of the skull with his fingertips. A large place on the back of the skull is sunken. Samiah looks across to the ruffled grass patches, then back to the body. "He was thrown here, and his head hit the ground when he landed; that is how he died," Samiah says.

"I have seen many dead men, yet I have never seen a corpse look as lifeless as this one," Aurick says.

"He looks deader than a dead man is supposed to look," a Rider comments, and his fellows nod in understanding.

"Yes, there is a look to him that is unnatural," Samiah agrees.

Then Inandaug asks, "What could have thrown him that far?"

No one answers.

"Search everywhere! Search the treetops, look for holes in the ground, anything!" Samiah shouts for all the men to hear. The Riders set out and Samiah trots to the brothers, sitting in wait. "Ghosts, search the river's edge, its waters; she is a good swimmer and may have used the river for escape. I am going to the bend where it slows. If she got out anywhere, it would have been there." Samiah's horse taps its hoof at the ground and Samiah looks down. His eyes catch a hint of shine. He slides from his horse and kneels to get a better look. The object is partially buried, so Samiah digs at the fresh dirt that covers it. He uncovers it and pulls it from the ground. Tears fill his eyes; it is Eramane's.

Samiah hears his parents arrive, and he dashes out of the house to greet them. He sees his mother first, her face marked with the unmistakable look of worry than can belong only to a mother. His father wears the burden as well, but his face also displays the exhaustion of harsh travels. The weather added to his parents' tough journey home, causing delay in their return.

The ground is saturated from heavy rains that began three days ago and have only recently ceased. The horses are dressed with mud up to their shoulders and haunches. The caretakers tend the carriage and horses, and Samiah walks behind his parents into the house where they last saw their daughter.

"Have you learned anything more?" Samiah's father asks, standing behind his wife, who sits in the brown leather chair, the wool wrap that warmed Eramane still draping the chair.

"We have searched tirelessly since we discovered she was gone." Samiah regrets not having anything more to tell his parents, regrets that he does not have their daughter.

"Did you find anything, son?" his father asks. Samiah swallows, deep and dry.

"Only these." He holds up Eramane's hair ribbon and the bird-wing hairpin.

"Oh, my poor child." His mother breaks into tears. She rises and buries her face in her husband's caring embrace.

"I am so sorry, Mother." Samiah's chin trembles. He walks across the room to his parents and takes both of them in his arms. "I am so sorry," he says again. He squeezes his father's shoulder, then breaks away. "I will find her," he proclaims and storms out of the house.

"Wait!" Mira shouts to her husband, who stops and turns. It has begun to rain again. "Where are you going, Samiah?"

"I am going to seek Lord Danius's counsel. Someone has to be able to help me find her, Mira."

She sees her husband's despair, rushes to him and holds him tight.

"You will find her, Samiah. She is still alive, I can feel it," Mira says. "Can you not?" she asks.

"Yes," he says faintly.

"Can you feel this?" Mira asks, placing her husband's hand on her belly. Samiah's eyes flicker from sorrow to hope.

"You are with child?" he asks, his eyes wide.

"Yes, love. Our baby is the reason for my recent bouts of illness," she admits. Samiah takes his wife in his arms and kisses her.

"You take care of yourself and our child. I will return soon." He bends down and kisses Mira's belly. "And you—stop making your mother so ill."

Mira watches from the shelter of the porch as her husband rides off, out of sight.

CHAPTER SEVEN

GRATITUDE

THE WATER IS HOT, AND steam rises from it, rolling over the edge of the stone tub. Adikiah's pile of furs was of no threat to me, as I had feared. Once he finished showing me the terrace where he sleeps, Adikiah led me back into the mountain, to the washing chamber, where I am now, soaking my dirt-stained skin and exhausted muscles. I imagine that my appearance was less than presentable. My hair is matted in some places with soil and small pieces of debris from the forest, and in others with snot and sweat.

The washroom has a large opening on the wall opposite the tub. I can see the stars when I look out. The full moon sends in its glow, making the flickering candles almost unnecessary. I plunge my head below the water and listen to the sounds in my mind that have been suppressed by the distractions of my new environment. At first I listen to the immediate sound, my heartbeat. It sounds the same as it did when I last bathed at

my brother's place. Then I hear the voices of my family: my
mother telling me to stay with her forever, my father's "I love
you" while he squeezed me good-bye, and Samiah's protective "When it comes to you, I do not trust any man." All of
their words play in my head like a song of comfort. But after
a while of listening to these soothing sounds, upset breaks
through, and my mother's and father's words turn into moans
and weeping, and Samiah's voice is no longer protective but
apologetic. I can hear him as if he were beside me: "I am sorry,
Eramane. I never should have let you go to the river." These
noises take over, and like a song memorized to the point of
madness, they are stuck in an unrelenting circle that plays over
and over, again and again.

My bath is no longer relaxing; I step out and wrap a robe
around me. I see a dress hanging on a metal bust, and I reach
for it. I hold up the garment left for me to wear. It is a deep
burgundy with gold embroidery in a pattern along the edges
of the sleeves and hem. A high collar stands up from the neck-
line, and black shiny gemstones form thin slanted lines along
its length. The dress is regal and extravagant and heavy. I put it
back on the wire frame and look around for my yellow dress.
Finding it lying on the floor next to the tub, I pick it up to
examine it. The skirt has a small tear, and it bears the stains
of grass and dirt in several places. I dip the soiled parts of
my yellow dress in the tub and scrub each spot until they are
all lightened, but somehow, because of the events that caused
them, the stains seem to stand out more than ever. I scrub
harder, but no amount of water and soap will erase them, just
as a bath and a beautiful burgundy gown cannot suppress my

memories of Lebis's death. I hold my dress to my face as I sob into it. I know that I should be grateful for Adikiah's hospitality, but I miss my home, and I know my family must be in agony wondering where I am, whether I am alive or dead. I need to go home and relieve them of their torment.

Finally, the stains are mostly gone, and I slide my dress on, taking comfort in its familiarity. I can do nothing for the small tear; it is hardly noticeable anyway. My foot is healing quite fast, faster than it should, really, and again I am grateful to Adikiah for that. "It is a special ointment; your foot will heal very soon," he said earlier when I asked him about the new bandages. I cannot reason with myself about my apprehension of telling Adikiah that I want to return to my home. He has never told me that I am a prisoner, has never treated me as a captive, but in my gut I feel that I am trapped here despite my wish to return home to my family. But I must tell him that I want to go.

"You do not like the gown I had placed in the washing chamber for you?" Adikiah asks, seeing that I am still in my yellow dress. He orders away the servant who escorted me to the terrace. We are alone there now; my eyes find the furs. I look away and find the courage to answer.

"I thought the dress was lovely," I say, giving him my honest opinion. My *most* honest opinion is that it is not something I would have chosen for myself.

"Yet you do not wear it." His speech is tight; I have offended him.

"Adikiah," I say, moving closer to him, "I do think the dress is lovely. But I do not feel that it is appropriate for me to accept such an extravagant gift. It looked as though it cost many coins." I see that my words have not changed his expression. He stands facing out toward the ocean; his feet only inches away from the ledge. I have been so concerned with having to tell him that I desire to leave, that I have not noticed the spectacular view. I walk over to the edge of the terrace and look down at the ocean. I cannot believe how high up we are. Adikiah's palace is on top of a mountain, surrounded by the ocean waters. I look in all directions. In the distance I see the shoreline; it looks like a hazy dark smear across the ocean's surface.

As I reach for his hand in an attempt to show my sincerity, his expression changes. His eyes are fixed on mine, and a hint of a smile graces his lips. My courage to tell him falters.

"I am not concerned with coin, Eramane. You are the singular thing that presses my thoughts," he says, his eyes content with having me in their gaze.

"I do not understand. Why am I a burden to you?" I ask. Adikiah takes my hand in his.

"You misunderstand me, Eramane. You are not a burden to me. I am concerned because I want you to like it here. I want you be happy here. I want you to stay here with me. Yet I see it in your face even now as you look at me; you wish to leave." Adikiah drops my hands and turns back to face the ocean. He wants me to stay with him. I am unsure of how to respond.

"Adikiah, I will never be able to repay you, or thank you enough, for saving me from that creature. I cannot imagine how you managed to defeat it. But you did; you saved me," I say. I hear the words aloud and realize how horribly ungrateful I will sound if I reject his offer to stay. He saved me. I am alive because this man risked his life to salvage my own; I owe him my life. Yet did he not intend to possess it anyway? Is that not what he meant when he said that he would come for me? "I want to see my family, to let them know that I am alive." His attention is back on me again.

"I brought you here to be with me, to fill my empty existence." He pauses briefly, then continues, "I will give you everything you have ever desired, and everything you do not yet know you want." He leans into my ear and whispers, "I will give you what your soul is ashamed to desire."

"Yes, you *brought* me here. Here, instead of my home. But I do not want to be here. I want to go home." I see his face tighten, his nostrils flare. "I cannot give you what you want, Adikiah. I do not feel love for you. I feel gratitude, beyond measure. That alone is not enough." I look to him for a reply. He stands motionless, his jaw clenched. I try to understand what he is feeling, why he chooses to remain silent. "I am sorry" is all I say. We both stand looking out over the ocean. It feels like an eternity of silence before Adikiah disrupts it.

"You are my not prisoner, Eramane. I will take you to your family. First, though, let your wounds heal, your body and mind recover. It is a long journey back."

CHAPTER EIGHT

THE TORBIUNS

"BRING THEM IN FOR JUDGMENT. They will be tried and condemned to the cells below Eludwid Hall," Lord Danius orders, pacing behind a large table, papers and maps of the territories strewn atop it. Samiah watches his lord, the ruler's face creased with hard lines and deep scars. He knows that Lord Danius has not finished. "Those Torbiuns have been running free far too long. I should have ended them when the opportunity was there." His voice lowers and his pace slows. "To think that they have your sister sickens me, Samiah." Lord Danius goes silent, his head turned toward correspondence on his council table. "This is one of hundreds of accusations against those hooligans." He looks up, a glimmer of excitement in his eyes. "They will not see the daylight if they live to be a hundred." He bellows a deep laugh.

"I will need enough Riders to help transport the clansmen back," Samiah says.

"Take as many as you need," Lord Danius offers.

"Thank you, Lord Danius," Samiah says, and he turns for the door.

"Samiah."

"Yes, my lord."

"Not one of those degenerates goes free," Lord Danius orders.

"My word," Samiah promises.

Samiah, the Ghosts, and twenty Riders make their way out of Eludwid and into the vast lands beyond the mountains. Terrin, Nahmas, and Aurick flank Samiah on each side. Since the riders have slowed their pace to let the horses rest, Terrin decides to move up next to Samiah and give his thoughts on their plan for invasion.

"Samiah," Terrin says in a low voice.

"What?"

"Have you considered the condition Eramane might be in if she has been a captive of the Torbiun clan?" Terrin asks.

"Of course I have, Terrin. It is all I can think of. And what's more disturbing is that I wish her to be alive when I know what being alive would mean for her. It makes my stomach turn. But praying that those disgusting Torbiuns have Eramane is the only hope I have."

"And if we do not find her at their camp?" Terrin asks.

"Then I will search for her until she is found or I take my last breath—whichever comes first," Samiah says, his heart heavy.

"Yes, High Commander," Terrin says and retreats to join his brothers.

Night has spread its dark blanket over the distant lands beyond Eludwid. Samiah halts his Riders just outside of the small Torbiuns camp, and after a tiresome journey where the days and nights melded together, Samiah and his Riders are in desperate need of rest. Nestled between the rock formations of nearby mountains, Samiah and his men discuss their plan of attack. Samiah and the Ghosts will go into the camp while the others surround it on foot, making sure none of their enemies escape. They will work their way through each dwelling, demanding the whereabouts of Eramane.

Samiah is unmatched with his sword and has perfected his skill with throwing knives. The Ghosts are a deadly team possessing great talent, and they are Samiah's most trusted companions. Nahmas specializes in throwing daggers, Terrin is a master of the bow, and Aurick uses powders and poisons in place of steel. The brothers are almost untouchable by any other man, and tonight they will assist Samiah in an attempt to rescue his sister.

The darkness cloaks Samiah and his Riders as they stalk the Torbiun camp. The clan numbers are less than two dozen, and if it were not for the matter of transporting the Torbiuns back, Samiah would have taken only the Ghosts in with him. Samiah stops to speak once more to the brothers before leading them into the camp. "No one escapes, understood?" The Ghosts nod in agreement and follow Samiah into the Torbiun camp. The brothers spread out a small distance from one another, leaving Samiah to invade up through the middle of the camp.

The smell of smoldering wood and old supper hangs heavy in the Torbiun campsite. Smoke lingers just above the ground and makes it difficult to see the sparsely scattered clansmen who are sleeping on the ground outside of shelters, but even the smoke shield does not protect the men from the Riders. Unfortunately, after questioning three men, the latter gain no knowledge of where Eramane might be.

Samiah reaches a draped area. Linens are tied up between trees; it is larger than the other shelters. *This must be where Ulic sleeps,* Samiah thinks to himself. Ulic is the leader of the Torbiun clan. Soon the Ghosts arrive to meet Samiah. He points to the dwelling, indicating to his men that Ulic is inside. Before entering the shelter, Samiah asks the brothers if they have gathered any information from the other Torbiuns.

"No, Samiah, it was a futile attempt; the men claimed to know nothing," Nahmas responds. Samiah puts his finger to his mouth, indicating for the Ghosts to be silent as they enter Ulic's shelter.

Ulic lies in what seems like a peaceful slumber. A woman next to him, unclothed and exposed, shivers in the night air. Food scraps litter parts of the ground that are not covered with armor and the half-naked woman's clothing. Ulic's snores fill

Samiah's ears, and he cringes at the thought of Eramane being Ulic's prize the night before. The camp does not contain any remnants of his sister or any clues to her whereabouts, but Samiah prays that Ulic will have the answer.

The woman rolls over to reach a nearby wool blanket. She momentarily opens her eyes and sees Samiah standing above her. She screams and grabs a nearby sword. The aimless woman clumsily lunges toward Samiah but is effortlessly disarmed and pushed to the ground. Ulic wakes from the disturbance, but Samiah is on top of him before he can rise from his bedding.

"Remember me?" Samiah puts his foot on Ulic's chest and forces him flat.

"I do," Ulic replies unafraid. Samiah clutches Ulic's head and forcefully demands him to stand. Ulic stands and shouts to alert his men of the danger. "Intruders!" he shouts.

"Your men are in no position to help you," Samiah declares, confident of his skilled Riders. Ulic is surprised by this news.

"What do you want, Samiah?" Ulic asks, nervousness in his voice.

"I believe you have my sister. The young woman you abducted from the meadow in Eludwid," replies Samiah.

"The young woman whose friend you murdered," Nahmas added. Ulic looks at Nahmas, until now unaware that the caster was in the shelter.

"You tell me where Eramane is right now," Samiah demands.

"Or what?" Ulic asks, understanding that the Riders are there to capture his clan, not kill them. "Somebody wants me alive; would it be Emach? What? Your noble lord tying up loose ends?" he mocks. Sweat saturates Ulic's round, scruffy face. "I have not seen your sister. Oh, and I bet she's pretty, just like her brother."

Samiah clenches his jaw and yanks Ulic away from the tree and into Nahmas's hands. "We are done here," Samiah says as he walks out of the dirty, smelly shelter.

Samiah and the Ghosts reunite with the other Riders. "We learned nothing of where my sister is. I do not know if Ulic is hiding the truth, but if he is, we will have to force it out of him when we get back to Eludwid." Samiah hangs his head and lowers his voice. "Where is my sister?" His tired eyes blink, heavy and slow. The thought of never finding Eramane centers in Samiah's thoughts. For the first time he recognizes the fact that she may be dead. This thought lashes at him, and he begins to find it difficult to hold himself together. "I need to be alone," Samiah insists as he jumps on his horse and walks his steed into the night. Nahmas follows a short distance behind. The mountain range is a dangerous place, especially when a man does not have his wits about him. Large predators occupy the range, and alone Samiah would be an easy target for a pack of wolves or mountain cats.

Samiah has not been on his ride for very long when he stops his steed. He is near a small village. The sounds of a celebration can be heard spilling from its happy hold.

"The Torbiuns were camped near this village. They must have

been planning to invade," Samiah says aloud. "We saved these
people from being attacked." His heart fills with happiness as
he absorbs the sounds of the celebration, knowing that the
villagers are safe from those foul Torbiun clansmen. Samiah
smiles as he tilts his head to face the stars. "At least I may have
saved these people." As he speaks, the guilt from Eramane's
disappearance stirs inside him and masks his feelings of joy.
Samiah commands his horse to proceed, but instead of obey-
ing him, the stallion begins scratching at the ground with its
front hoof. Samiah looks down and sees the reason for his
steed's disobedience.

CHAPTER NINE

THE GLASS TOMB

I WAKE FROM THE SOUND of thunder. For a short time, I look up into the seemingly endless nothing above me. Adikiah ordered his servants to provide me with a proper bed so that my stay is more comfortable. I am thinking about the past few days I have been here with Adikiah. He has been at my side every moment, and I have become fond of his company. He has told me stories of far-off lands, some of which I have never heard of. He told me of a place where the air is so cold it forms an ice bridge that is so long you cannot see to the other end, and that when the warm weather comes, the bridge melts; if you have crossed to the other side, you will be trapped there until it freezes back. Of these far-off lands, my favorite is the underwater cavern. Adikiah said that there is a place underneath the ocean that opens up to air. I listened in disbelief as he described the span of the cavern, large enough to build a town in. He says that he is the only one to know of this cavern, because he can hold his breath longer than any man, and you must be able to hold it for a good length of time before reaching the cavern. "It is just beyond those rocks," he said, pointing to a small cluster of protruding boulders, not far from the mountain palace.

Not all of Adikiah's stories are of frozen bridges and underwater towns. Last evening, he told me of his life, how he had no family, no one to share time with. His words were somber, barely uttered when he spoke of the torment in his solitude. "Why do you live this way?" I asked.

"There was no other way, until you, Eramane." Until me? His answer filled me with dread, the burden of an assumed commitment. And this is where my thoughts land as I look up into the dark.

The daylight spills through the large window across from me as I dress. After offending Adikiah by refusing the burgundy gown, I decided to wear the items he placed in the washing chamber for me. Yet these garments are not extravagant like the gown; they are simpler, like my yellow dress. I choose a pale green dress with long sleeves; it is cold in the mountain palace. As soon as I exit my chamber, I see Adikiah. He waits for me each day and walks me to the dining chamber. I am not very hungry this morning. Sadness has set in my belly, replacing the feeling of hunger. I miss my parents, Samiah and Mira, my home. What is more unsettling is that I have come to feel that I belong here, that fate brought me here for a specific purpose. Yet becoming Adikiah's wife seems a detail outside of fate's plans. I have tried to imagine myself as his companion, but my heart still pines for Lebis, and as long as it does, there is not room enough for anyone else.

Adikiah sits in quiet while I pick at the berries on my plate. "What troubles you this morning, Eramane?" he asks. I do not wish to answer, but my words come out easily, despite my desire for them not to.

"I feel better now, Adikiah. My foot has been healed completely for some time now, and my bruises and lacerations were never anything to be concerned about," I say, stopping to gauge his reaction. He sits expressionless, staring at me. Finally he speaks.

"Let me show you something," he replies. He slides his chair in a quick motion that sends a loud screech throughout the chamber. I stand, more delicately than he, and walk over to him; his hand is outstretched, as it is most times.

We enter a chamber, lit only by the flame of a single torch. We have no sooner entered when a servant moves from behind us and to the unlit torches that remain. The servant is quiet and swift; the room is bright in a matter of seconds, revealing an abundance of relics: body armors inlaid with gold script, statues of men bearing different crests, swords larger than any I have ever seen, crowns of various shapes and sizes, insects modeled out of gold and jewels. But what holds my attention is what lies in the large glass case in the middle of the room.

I cannot stop myself from clutching Adikiah's arm and burying my face in his back. He peels me from his arm so that he can enfold me in both of them. "Do not be afraid, Eramane; it is dead," he assures me, releasing me from his embrace so that I can look for myself. My trembling body objects as I make my way to the glass coffin. My legs feel as if someone else is trying to control them, trying to direct them away from the fragile-looking tomb. I reach it and find myself amazed that Adikiah possesses it. Not inches from me, sealed in glass, are the remains of the beast that murdered Lebis and tried to murder me. Its long, hardened body resembles the lifeless statues of the men bearing crests. The wings of the beast wrap around it, making a cocoon. Even in its death, the creature still looks fierce, frightening … able.

"How did you do this, Adikiah? How did you kill this thing and bring it back here?" I ask, running my hand over the top of the glass. "You are one man."

"I am, but one man can have many resources."

"Your servants?" I ask.

"They are useful in many ways, yes," he says. My gaze does not leave the entombed beast. As I stare at it, my memories of the meadow surge through me. I feel my body begin to quake, and rage consumes me. I slam my fists on the surface of the case, and it splits under the impact. I do not realize I am screaming at the corpse until Adikiah covers my mouth with his palm. "It is all right, Eramane. He cannot hurt you," he says, trying to comfort me. I release my tears on his chest and keep my face hidden until I can catch my breath.

"Thank you," I tell him, not believing that could ever be enough. He lifts my face to look at me.

"Stay with me, Eramane," his soft words ask. "Become my companion, and we will travel to the distant lands whence these relics came. Your life will be filled with experiences from the farthest reaches of this world. I will keep you safe, from even the fiercest of things," he says, and his eyes move from me to his encased trophy.

"My debt to you can be repaid only by an agreement of marriage?" I ask.

"You owe me nothing, Eramane. Our union would make me happy, but only if it brings you happiness as well."

I want to make him happy, and I know that I can grow to love him one day, but I fear that once I return home to see my family, I will not want to leave again.

"I need to lie down." I do not know what else to say. Adikiah escorts me to my chamber, where I find the bed to be extra welcoming. He says nothing before leaving, the rattling of the door filling in for unspoken words.

CHAPTER TEN

THE CATALYST

"THEY WILL BE displeased with your actions, gatekeeper." A cauldron of black, frothing liquid is the catalyst of the clicking, fluttering voice speaking to Adikiah. He keeps the cauldron in the chamber where the Gate is, deep in the subregions of the palace.

"They should be pleased with what I have to offer them. The blood of a summoner is worth more to them than a thousand souls," Adikiah fires back to the voice that angers him.

"In all of eternity, she will not forgive you for this. Her memory will only be disrupted temporarily, and then you will have to explain yourself," the voice says, fueling Adikiah's anger.

"When she *becomes* and is like me, once she harvests, she will understand; there will be no need for explanations." Adikiah grabs the edges of the cauldron. "She will *know* me," he finishes.

"What if she is not like you? This has never been done before, and to a summoner. There are no guarantees, no comparative accounts," it says.

"She will be like me. I can see it in her eyes. I can feel it!" Adikiah rages.

"And if the Orders of the Reach do not accept her blood, if they want her soul instead?"

"Then she will die!" Adikiah's tone softens at the idea. "I will not give her up to them." Adikiah peers at his reflection in the shiny, thick liquid. He shakes the bowl and disrupts his appearance in its contents; turning from it he says, "They will accept my offering, or they shall never receive another harvest!" The voice in the cauldron does not stifle its amusement; its throaty chuckle sends the liquid into a boil.

"When shall I retrieve your offering?" The voice from the black liquid is excited; its words crackle and click rapidly.

"When the next moon if full," Adikiah says. "She will be ready when the next moon is full.

CHAPTER ELEVEN

THE CREVICE

ADIKIAH WAKES ME; it is the first time he has entered my sleeping chamber. "Come with me, Eramane." Adikiah's eyes gleam with excitement—or hysteria, I cannot tell which—and I have come to dread those words: "Come with me, Eramane." The last time he spoke them, he took me to the room where the dead beast lay. Yet I follow him, down the staircase to a chamber in the palace. A deep crevice makes a barrier between the entrance and the back of the room and casts an orange glow throughout the chamber. The walls and the floor are dark and slick, reflecting the pulsing orange radiance seeping from the crevice

"Why have you brought me down here?" I ask.

"I need to reveal something to you." He looks at the opening in the floor, and pulls me close to the crevice. "You see, Eramane?" He motions for me to look down. Molten earth churns below, and the heat rushes my face. I step back. "I can do many things, defeat armies and bring their weapons and armor and idols home with me." He places his finger on my forehead. "But I cannot summon the earth as you can."

"What do you mean?" I ask, utterly dismayed by his accusation.

"I am telling you that you have a gift, Eramane, a magnificent one." My head will not stop shaking in rejection.

"Gift, as in magic? Are you serious?" is my reply.

"Yes, Eramane. Look at the crevice. You can close or spread its girth, whichever you choose."

"I do not believe you. You are mad."

"And this gift is why I cannot let you go home," he says.

"Let me go home?" I feel my body begin to heat. "You said I was not your prisoner; you said you would take me home."

"Yes, but I am only trying to protect you, Eramane. If you return and your lord discovers your secret, who knows what he will have done with you?"

"He will have nothing done with me! I am no summoner. You are lying!"

A slender figure enters the room, a servant. It holds a silver goblet. Adikiah takes the cup from his servant but does not order it away. "I am not making false claims, Eramane," he says and shoves the servant over the ledge into the crevice.

"Why did you do that?" I ask in awe. Adikiah orders other servants to enter; four more take positions next to their master.

"I am proving to you that you can control this crevice," he says, pushing a second over the ledge.

"Stop!" I plead. His shoves a third over. "Please, Adikiah, stop killing them!" He does not seem to care about my request. I feel that familiar quaking that surges through me as my anger reaches its climax. A fourth is sacrificed. "No more!" I scream and the ground begins to tremble, the chamber walls to quake. I expel the rage inside me and gasp when I see the crevice start to open wider. My amazement halts my fit, and instantly the earth ceases movement. The fifth servant is ordered out.

"Well, that was not the intended direction, but look, Eramane, see what you did?" I am breathless and cannot speak. "And your eyes, they glow so magnificently, like the brightest of moons," he says. He slowly walks toward me, cup still in hand.

"I am leaving," I say, turning for the door. "I do not need your help to get home."

"Eramane, wait!" he orders. I halt at the powerful command. "There is no need for you to be angry. If you still wish to go home, I will take you. But please, drink this to calm yourself. I do not want you bringing down my palace." I turn back to him, take the cup, and put it to my lips. It goes down easy, leaving a sweet aftertaste.

In seconds my body goes numb, and Adikiah catches me before I collapse to the floor. What is happening?

I am aware of my surroundings, only I cannot move or speak. Adikiah has taken me to the terrace, where he has laid me on the floor. He holds my head in his arms; his expression reveals his excitement. But there is something else behind his eyes: fear, remorse, guilt—any of the three fits perfectly. Then he leans in close to me and whispers, "I have to kill you, my love." I try to scream aloud, but my body is under siege by the toxin Adikiah gave me. Tears stream down my face. At least I can show him my tears.

"Do this for me, Eramane. Make me whole. End my loneliness, and you will have everything you have ever dreamed of. I will worship you and no other with more passion than the sun has for burning. You will be mine, and I will be yours—forever," he claims passionately.

Adikiah moves to the edge of the terrace. He looks to the skies and spreads his arms, holding his head high, clenching his hands into fists. The wind grows stronger. He turns and hurries over to me. The winds are boisterous. Strong gusts blow through the veranda. Adikiah grabs my shoulders and commands my full attention.

"Eramane, it is time!" he shouts over the roaring winds. "Do not be afraid, my love; it will be over soon!" As he speaks, his handsome body begins to contort into his true form. His face stretches from the bones of his skull enlarging. His tan skin grows darker until it is almost black, like a slate stone. The sound of his bones breaking is softened by the loud wind. In a matter of seconds he grows taller, and huge horns coil out from above his brow. Then his long, leathery wings sprout, stretching out several feet on each side of his body. Adikiah never saved me from any beast; he is the beast. He leans over and lifts me into his arms with no effort, and once again I am in the arms of the horrifying creature.

We fly to the top of the terrace, where he places me on my back. Adikiah turns to the sky and begins chanting words I have never heard before, and the winds distort them. I cannot make them out, but as he speaks, the sky changes color: from black, to dark blues, to deep reds and purples. Lightning pulses and pierces through the montage of colors in the sky. Adikiah turns and walks over to me. He takes hold of my body, pulling me close. I focus on his eyes; they are locked on mine. "I love you, Eramane. I am sorry." He rakes his sharp claws down the center of my arm, and I can only watch as my blood drains into a metal canister.

After a short while, my body begins to convulse, and I have no breath to scream. Adikiah sets me down and holds the metal canister containing my blood up to the heavens that have ceased changing color and are fixed in a deep crimson.

"Come and claim your offering!" he shouts, blood trickling down his forearm. Adikiah sets the canister down on the terrace top. Adikiah has summoned evil to his mountaintop. Screams pierce my ears as an entity, smelling of death and looking like the gathering of all the bugs of the earth, comes twisting and coiling from the sky. The dark mass of demise reaches us and settles just above me, hovering, looking at my body as if it wants to devour me. A face forms on this ungodly thing and speaks to me. In a clicking, cracking, low mumble, it says, "So you are the summoner." Its face contorts as it speaks. I gaze into the eyes of this being, watching them turn to fire. It looks at me, laughing maniacally. The laugh grows stronger, more intense, but the monstrosity moves away from me to fetch the blood-filled canister.

"Take it and leave!" Adikiah commands. "I have given you what they need! Leave *now!*" he screams at the writhing body. Taking heed of Adikiah's command, the creature twists its way down to the canister and grasps it with its gnarled teeth. Securing the offering, the demonic creature flies away into the red abyss. I can no longer see it, yet I hear it laughing. Eventually the laughter grows faint and then vanishes.

I can scream now, and I do. My screams seem to have been the sign Adikiah is waiting for. "It is time for you to *become*, my love." He lays me on my back again and leans over, putting his mouth to mine. I stare into Adikiah's eyes as he begins breathing his own life into me. Adikiah stands up and backs away from my body. I shake vigorously, thrashing around like a fish washed ashore, and I begin spitting up thick, tarlike muck. Adikiah rushes to my side and wipes my mouth.

"It worked, my love! We are the same now! We are one." His voice staggers as he speaks. Lifting me, Adikiah brings me back down and places me in his bedding. I fall into the grips of sleep, taking the impish, distorted face with me.

ERAMANE'S HARVEST

"ERAMANE, WAKE UP," ADIKIAH ASKS of me. I wake just as the sun sets, leaving only its reflections of pink in the dark blue dusk. I squint as I look around; the faint hint of daylight that remains intrudes on my eyes, sending piercing bright flashes across my sight. I stand and walk to the edge of the terrace, trying to gain control of my vision. I look down toward the ocean, and in between the flashes of white I am able to make out details on the ocean floor: sand swirling as waves move above it, ocean life darting in and out of their homes, the stripes on a fish that swims along the reef. Looking back to the horizon, my eyes take me miles from the mountain palace, yet the long-sightedness is not settling well in my stomach. My belly turns and images of my surroundings circle around me. I become dizzy and almost collapse, but Adikiah catches me and seats me on the stone ledge. The images slow and I fix my gaze on Adikiah; through his clothing and his flesh, I see inside his body. He has no heart and no blood courses through his veins; a faint red glow pulsates in the center of his core, and nothing more.

He seems to be the only thing I am familiar with, other than the mountain palace. I rise to stand, using Adikiah's arm to steady myself.

"Relax, Eramane. You will adjust to your new eyes. Welcome these senses," he advises as he looks me over with wonder and amazement. "What a marvel you have become," he adds.

"Become?" Anxious to see what he is speaking of, I walk to a mirror. Staring at my reflection, I do not recognize any difference or any familiarity. I gaze longer; I am not certain of my reflection. It is as if I am looking at a stranger, yet only because my memory of myself is vague. I look at my long, dark red hair, lightly bronzed skin, and eyes the color of a golden sunset. My memory loss brings a rise of concern. I turn to Adikiah. "Why can I not remember myself?"

"Your memory will return soon enough," he says.

"What happened? Did I have an accident?" I wait for his reply.

"No, Eramane, you did not," he says.

"Well what, then? Why am I able to remember only you— and this place?" I lift my arm, motioning to the terrace; I feel a weight pull on my back. I turn my head to get a look. "What is that?" I scream, frightened at the sight of the velvety black wing protruding from my back. I look to the other side; it has a match. "Adikiah, why do I have wings?" I scream at him, knowing his words will not console me.

"Are they not beautiful?" Adikiah seems to be taken by them, like an envious child who covets the new toy of another.

"What has happened to me?" I blink tears from my eyes so I can see him.

"You have *become*, Eramane," he explains. I rush back to the mirror and turn to view the wings; they droop to the floor under their own weight, like the long braches of a willow tree. "What have you done to me?" My voice is shrill and frantic. I cannot stop my tears.

"You must harvest, Eramane. Once you do, you will feel more like yourself."

I no longer give him my attention; the wings on my body own the entirety of my interest. They are unnatural and no amount of time will ever make them feel a part of me. The longer I stare at them, the more I weep, and at last I am sent into an uncontrollable fit. I grab the top of one of the wings and try with all of my might to tear it from my body. Pieces of velvety sheath slide underneath my fingernails as I try remove them from me.

"Eramane, stop!" Adikiah shouts, running up to me. He grabs my hands and forces them down, but to my amazement, and his, I easily break his grip and reach again for the wings. "Stop! You will hurt yourself!" he commands, but his words mean nothing, and I will not stop until the wings are no longer attached to me.

He tries again to control my hands; I push him and he staggers back a few feet away from me. Before he comes to a stop, a flux in his appearance captures my full attention. His face and body bulge and begin changing color. Slate pigments ripple across his skin, consuming all of the bronzed flesh. His eyes burn orange, like the fires in the palace, and bones push out of his forehead; undulating until they form thick, coiled shields on each side of his head. On his back, wings unfold and flex out several feet around him and above him, displaying a bluish-purple sheen, like that of a black snake in the midday sun. His height increases by three or four feet, and in a matter of seconds, Adikiah's image settles. A dark-hided, winged beast stands before me.

Adikiah rushes me and pins me to a stone column. "Stop, Eramane," he huffs. I am in awe of his transformation, yet I am not afraid of him. Instead, his order enrages me. I push against him, finding it difficult to move him. He is much stronger in this beast state; I push harder. He shoves back and now his face is in mine, his eyes locked on mine. "I will not let you do this," he says.

I peer into his fire-colored eyes, and images of trees and a meadow flash before me. Confusion and distrust overwhelm me. I summon every ounce of strength I have and give another shove; I move him off of me, and, taking advantage of the small space of freedom between us, I leap from the terrace. My wings spread out, fierce and glorious, the moonlight reflecting off their velveteen coat, and I disappear into the darkness. Adikiah does not follow.

Adikiah looks out at the ocean; the moon, still round and luminous, shines onto the black ocean waters, making it appear as if silver snakes slither along its surface. He has held his beast form, apparently unable to decide whether he wants to go in search of his companion. "Where have you gone?" he asks aloud, eyes scanning the skies. A flutter from behind reaches his ears, and he turns toward it. "I did not expect you back so soon," he says, relieved.

I hit the stone terrace top with such control that I feel as if I stepped onto it after walking down a flight of stairs. My grace impresses Adikiah and a faint smile bares his sharp teeth.

"Where else am I supposed to go?" I ask. "Out there, nothing is familiar, welcoming. This is the only place I feel I belong," I say, in a tone of mild disgust. Adikiah remains where he is, but I see his muscles flinch as he fights the urge to approach me. "What are you? I ask.

"I am the gatekeeper. I harvest the souls of men."

"Harvest—why?" I ask, unable to determine why a soul would need to be harvested.

"So that we may live," he says, his voice still.

"I am alive!" I shout, relieving only a portion of my harnessed anger.

"For now, yes, but if you do not harvest, you will die," he replies calmly.

"And what does that mean, to harvest?" I ask.

"To take the essence of a human and absorb it into your body. It nourishes us, Eramane."

"This kills them?" My voice trembles at the thought of his reply being yes, and tears break forth when he confirms it.

"It does," he says. I look away from him and walk to the edge of the terrace top. I will not kill to live; I would rather die. I look down at the waves as they crash against the rocks at the bottom of the mountain.

"I could jump," I say.

"I would catch you before you reached the bottom," Adikiah says softly, and I know he would.

"It is a brutal way to live," I say, still looking down at the crashing waves.

"Is the lion brutal when it takes down its prey? I am an animal just the same. We are all animals, Eramane, are we not? Humans slaughter one another over power, greed, fear … is that not brutal? The variations of death do not matter. I did not choose to be a gatekeeper, but it is my fate and has been for centuries. If not for me, the Orders of the Reach would spew from this mountain like the hot molten rock from its belly. Life upon life would be consumed until nothing was left, yet humankind does not show me gratitude; instead they hunt me." Adikiah falls silent and I reflect on his words, taking in all he has told me.

I wake from the midday sun warming my skin. I slept on the terrace top; it is the only place I do not feel confined. Adikiah must have covered me during the night; I did not have a pelt blanket when I curled up on the hard stone. I have now adjusted well to my vision; the images no longer make me unsteady. It is the first time I have really seen without feeling dizzy.

Adikiah has come to join me; I hear the pebbles on the terrace top rattle as he lands, and I look over my shoulder to acknowledge his presence. He changes into his human form before approaching. "I prefer your true form," I say, my jaw tight, my sight fixed to the horizon.

"You do?" He is surprised by my preference.

"Yes. Why should you be able to hide your afflictions, yet I must bear mine?"

"You see this as an affliction?" he asks, offended, but remains placid.

I say nothing. It is a difficult transition; he must understand that.

"Eramane." His voice softens. "I am sorry you have been so devastated by this. It was not supposed to be so difficult for you. Look at me." He gently places his hands on my shoulders and turns me to face him. "You will move beyond this, but you must harvest, or you will die."

My despair dwindles upon his touch. Once his hands brush against my skin, I feel a transfer of emotion from him, as if he were telling me his thoughts. I can feel what he feels when he looks at me; I am not an object under his will, like the servants that bend to his demands. I am his only reason for living; yet even this is not enough to change my mind. I will not harvest, and this is how I will die, finding peace in my death.

I wake up to the darkness. I sit up and look around the terrace. My vision has blurred and I can see only to the edges of the terrace-top landing. I try to stand, but I am weak. I am unsure of how long it has been since my *becoming*, but my skeletal shape indicates that it has been long enough for starvation to take hold. I gauge my decline by the amount of velvet that has shed from my wings; strips of the soft coating hang from them, as moss hangs from trees. My mouth is dry and my lips have cracked beyond the point of bleeding. After several attempts I manage to stand, and although I cannot see very far, I know exactly where Adikiah is. In moments he will land on the terrace, presenting a third human offering. I will refuse and he will shout to the heavens, begging that something more powerful than he can persuade me to harvest.

I stumble to the ledge and look toward the ocean rocks, a recently acquired habit. I can see nothing but darkness. Only a short time ago I would have been able to watch as different-colored fish swam around: yellow ones, blue ones, black and orange ones. I could have seen the ocean plants, coral, and the white sand at the bottom—everything. My hazy recollection is disturbed.

"Eramane, it is time." Adikiah's voice is unlike I have heard it before. A renewed confidence resonates in his words.

"To harvest?" I let out a dry laugh, which blends with a choking cough. He places an unconscious body before me. Just as I did with the previous two, I turn away from it.

"Eramane, your refusal will cost two lives this time."

I turn to him and see that he holds a small child in his arms; a young girl—two, maybe three months in age. He looks down to the ocean rocks, and I know what he means to do with the child if I do not harvest. My will is broken. I am not sure if my desire to live or the desire to save the child is the cause for my giving in, but the strength I had to die has vanished.

I move to the limp body, not knowing what to do with the young man when I reach him. Adikiah sees that I struggle with the process and bends down to aid me, laying the small child on the stone.

"Like this," he says, grasping the man's head while clutching his throat. Adikiah rips the body away and tosses it behind us. What remains in Adikiah's grip is a thin, featureless white glow the length of the victim. "Place your palm on his chest," Adikiah explains. I do as he says; my hand sinks into the mass. It feels warm and malleable, like the filling of a fruit pie fresh from a brick oven. I watch thin lines, the same white glowing color, trace up my arm. As they enter my core, a feeling washes over me; I feel light and numb and exhilarated at once.

I lie flat on the stone floor, letting the energy course through me. It tingles as it surges, but the process does not last long. I sit up and look to Adikiah. He is pleased and relieved. "You look strong again, Eramane."

"I feel strong again," I say. "Now return that child to its parents," I say. Contempt is strong in my voice, and Adikiah knows that I will never forgive him for his manipulation.

Adikiah did as I requested; he took the child away hours ago. I have not left the landing yet; maybe I never will. I crossed a line by accepting the harvest, and I can never go back. If I refuse another offering, Adikiah will only threaten the life of another innocent. What is left is the challenge of accepting my new life and everything that it encompasses. I think about leaving, but where would I go? I do not know where I came from, whether I have a family. Could I find a mountain of my own, safe from kings' armies? Maybe, but none of this means anything; after learning of Adikiah's feelings for me, I know that he will follow me wherever I go. I will never be free of him.

Adikiah has chosen a place for us to harvest. We stand on the landing, he in his true form, an obsidian sentinel, and I an unassuming predator. "Vegamon is northwest of here. Our journey will be long, but the harvest will justify the distance," he says, his chest heaving with the eagerness of our first harvest together. "It benefits us to harvest farther from the mountain; it keeps the humans away from our shores," he adds. My wings extend without my mind's command; they act on their own, as if they know I am about to leap from the landing. Adikiah takes to the air first, I only seconds behind.

Soaring through the night, I take advantage of my heightened vision. I can see miles ahead and every insect that buzzes by. I watch animals scurry along the ground below, following their beating hearts until they have gone beyond my vision. I am still in awe of my abilities.

We have traveled for the first half of the night, but now we close in on the village of Vegamon. Snow coats the ground, and mist from the mountains empties from the bellies of the large rocks. The air has cooled drastically, and I watch puffs of my own breath turn into tiny, glittering, frozen droplets. As I play with my breath and the freezing air, I notice that something falls from above us. Adikiah is unaware at first, and I look up to see if anything else is coming down. As I scan the heavens, Adikiah takes part in the investigation.

"Did you see it too?" I ask.

"No," Adikiah replies. "I can hear it, though," he finishes. We continue searching the sky, and then I hear the sound of the falling objects. It is similar to the sound of a spear being thrown past one's ear, cutting the air with ease—a low, whooshing sound. More of the mysterious objects begin to fall, plummeting uncomfortably close to us. Adikiah sees them now, and we can determine that large shards of frozen water are these spears that stab at us from above. One nearly clips my right wing.

"What is going on?" I ask.

"I am not sure," Adikiah replies. At first the icy daggers are few, but their presence soon increases, and after only a moment, they rain down on us with fierce velocity.

Adikiah dives for the protection of the trees, knowing that I will follow. As we pass through the forest, shards of wood fly out at us. The frozen spears are ripping small trees in half, sending large wooden splinters in all directions. "We are under attack!" Adikiah yells back to me. "We must get back out into the open!" he exclaims. As we swoop through the forest and near our exit, one of the frozen shards pierces my shoulder, knocking me out of the air and to the ground with a forceful impact.

"No!" Adikiah bellows. He turns and twists, trying to dodge the attack. He is slashed several times by both wooden and ice shards before he reaches me. "It will be all right, Eramane! I will get you out of here—just hold on!"

Again I am pierced, this time through my left wing, and it is just as painful as the shoulder hit. I see worry in Adikiah's expression; does he doubt our escape? My strength dwindles, and I do not know how much more of this assault I can handle.

As more frozen stakes plummet toward us, I see desperation on Adikiah's face to get us out of there. He reaches for me, but before his fingers touch my skin, a shard of wood from a tree pierces through my leg and into the ground, pinning me there. Adikiah cries out in frustration.

The ground begins to tremble and crack, and Adikiah turns from me to investigate the quake. Dust from the earth clouds our vision and blinds us for a moment. Through the haze I see giant claws tearing away at the ground, and something begins to pull itself up from the dirt. When the dust settles, we see what has crawled out of the earth.

It is an enormous creature, slightly larger than Adikiah. Black fur covers the beast. Long claws and fangs make up its weapons. The beast looks like a giant feline with knobby, horn-like bones protruding between its ears, like the newly growing horns of a bull calf. There are many of these structures on top of its head, which allows the beast to ram its victims with great force. The eyes of this monster are wide sockets of green with a vertical black center, and its fangs drop out of its mouth, hanging below its bottom jaw.

Soon this beast will attack, and I will witness the extent of Adikiah's might. The ice crystals, still falling all around us, pierce me again. This time one goes through my hand, and I shriek in agony. Torment grows inside Adikiah as he witnesses this brutal assault. I am growing weak, but I have the strength to remove the shard from my hand. Gripping the wooden dagger, I give a quick yank, and the stake is removed, but not without sharp pain and a loud scream. I look to Adikiah; the behemoth feline has his full attention.

The stocky creature jumps at Adikiah and takes a crouching position in front of him. Adikiah picks up two large wooden shards from the ground. He stands guarded, trying to anticipate the creature's actions. The feline beast lunges at Adikiah and wraps its paws around him, sending them both to the ground, the beast on top. It covers Adikiah almost completely, and I cannot imagine that Adikiah has not be crushed under its weight. I helplessly look on as nothing else happens. The creature is motionless, and I fear that Adikiah is dead. This should fill me with joy; if Adikiah dies, I can die too. But I find that this fact does not bring happiness to me. Instead I feel a faint prickle of dread; if Adikiah dies, then I die—and I no longer wish for death! Just as I reach the point of real fright, I see small movements from the feline beast, as if it is trying to stand. After a few moments, I see that it is Adikiah pushing the creature off of him. Adikiah lets out a forceful grunt as he shoves the dead beast onto its side. Two stakes pierce its chest.

"This is going to hurt," Adikiah says. He grasps the ice shard that has me pinned to the ground. I take a deep breath, and he pulls it from my leg. An agonized scream surges out of me. Adikiah tosses the shard aside and lifts me into his arms. Again we are flesh to flesh, and I can feel what he feels: remorse.

"I will take you home, my love," he promises. I feel as though I will not make it there; I am completely numb … no pain, no fear, nothing. He sweeps me into the air, and we fly above the trees.

"Adikiah, I'm dying," I say softly. My lust to live has faded, and I am ready to die.

"You do not think those things, Eramane! You are mine!" Adikiah commands as we soar above the earth. "You do not worry about death! It cannot harm us! Do you understand me?" He descends and we slam to the ground harshly, but with control. "You will not die, Eramane," Adikiah declares as he places me on the ground. We are near a village, and I can hear people celebrating something, a wedding maybe, a funeral possibly. I do not know. "I will return soon. You must harvest," he says, kissing my dry lips. He leaves and I am alone in the darkness.

꧁

My body is shaken alive by a force that is not my own. I wake and watch as a limp body lands on the ground next to me. "Take it, Eramane; it will make you stronger," Adikiah says eagerly. I look at this person lying beside me; she is a young woman with long blonde hair. Tear streak her cheeks. For a moment I wonder to whom this stranger belongs; someone loves her. Maybe she is the mother of a cheerful little boy, and his only joy in life is playing at the river with his mother and father. She could be the sister to a very proud brother, who boasts of her to all his friends. And maybe her existence is solely for the purpose of saving my life. I look over at Adikiah; his arms are empty.

Everything my new life encompasses … this means I must harvest to live; if I do not take the girl's life, I will die, and Adikiah can do nothing to stop it. I do not see another innocent with him; could he not find a second human?

My instinct to survive takes over; the stranger has to die for me to live. I crawl a short distance to her and grab her by her neck. She moans when I clasp her head, yet again I am unable to extract the soul, my hand still mangled from the shard that pierced it earlier. Adikiah approaches and prepares her soul for me; my palm sinks into her chest, and the white glowing lines climb up my arm.

The energy shoots through my body like a rushing river. I feel myself healing from the wounds of the ice shards. The gashes repair themselves before my eyes; the deep lacerations are not as gruesome, but they are still visible.

"You see why it is so important for us to harvest? As long as we have strength, we are untouchable," Adikiah says, happily watching me gain in strength. I understand completely now. I feel different, even more so than after my first harvest. I feel carnal, lustful, like I fulfilled an ultimate desire.

"Adikiah, I can fly now. Let us go from here before the villagers discover us. I do not wish another attack," I say. Adikiah lifts into the air; I jolt up behind him.

CHAPTER THIRTEEN

Mountains End

LYING AT THE FEET OF Samiah's horse is the corpse of a woman. Samiah swallows. He fears that the body might be Eramane; from up on his horse he cannot be sure. He slides slowly down the side of his horse, staring straight ahead into dark nothingness. Samiah kneels down to the body and, reaching for the dead woman, begins to pray that she is not his sister. The corpse is still warm, but there does not yet appear to be a cause to her death. Samiah looks up to the dark heavens. "Please do not let this be my sister. Please do not let this be my sweet Eramane," he begs. He gets closer to see whether the woman is in fact Eramane. Rolling her over, he is still unsure; her hair has matted to her face. Samiah eagerly moves away the hair until he sees that the dead woman is not his sister. His chest heaves as he sighs in relief.

Looking down at the body again, Samiah is reminded of Lebis's corpse. Samiah feels the back of her head and finds the same type of wound on her that he found on Lebis. He backs away from the body in awe. "What did this to you?" he asks the dead woman. "I hope the same fate did not find my sister." Samiah mounts his horse and proceeds toward the festive village. He is confused and does not understand how no one heard the screams from the woman. "Even with all the music, they should have heard her screams," he contemplates aloud. Noise comes from behind Samiah and halts his thoughts.

"My apologies, High Commander, but I could not let you venture out here alone," Nahmas says, riding up to meet Samiah. Samiah is grateful of his following but looks around for the rest of the Riders.

"Where are the others?" Samiah asks.

"I ordered them back to Eludwid. The Torbiun clansmen do not need the advantage of our delay," Nahmas explains, knowing that his High Commander will agree. "Terrin and Aurick will await our arrival at Eludwid Hall."

"Well then, it is just you and me. Let's go find out what happened to this girl." Samiah turns his horse in the direction of the village.

"It is a dreadful thing, but I am glad she is not your sister," Nahmas comments as he looks back at the dead woman.

"Someone had to have seen something," Samiah says as they both walk their horses into the village.

"Mountains End," Samiah reads from a small wooden sign that hangs from a torch post. Lights cast a warming glow to fill the pathways of the small settlement. The dwellings in this village are close together and form a barrier for each side of the dirt path. As the two men slowly ride their horses through the village, the people begin to stop their festivities and look at the newcomers. Soon the two-piece band no longer plays, and the children stop their games. When all grows quiet, Samiah speaks loud enough to be heard by all the villagers: "My name is Samiah Fahnestock; this is my comrade Nahmas. We are Riders for Lord Emach Danius. Amidst your fun and games a woman was attacked and lies dead just outside the wooded area behind your village." As his words reach the ears of the townspeople, they all begin to look around to see who is missing. Moments later, a woman begins shouting about her lost daughter.

"Thea! I cannot find Thea." The sobbing woman runs up to Samiah and grabs him. "Is it my Thea? Is it?" she demands.

"I do not know, my lady," Samiah says to her, shaking his head. The frightened woman dashes to the woods.

Samiah looks around at the townspeople and notices a young boy, about ten years old, standing silent on the stoop of a home. He was not among the townsfolk when Samiah and Nahmas first arrived. The boy came out from inside the dwelling and focused his stare in the direction of the dead woman. Samiah alerts Nahmas to the boy on the stoop, although Nahmas has already noticed him. They both dismount their steeds and walk slowly over to the boy, as townsmen arm themselves and rush into the woods. Samiah looks around for the boy's parents. "What is your name, boy? Where are your mother and father?" Samiah asks.

"I thought I imagined it," says the boy, ignoring Samiah's questions. As he speaks, Samiah and Nahmas listen intently. "I thought if I went inside, it would all go away. Everyone celebrated still, so I thought that it did not happen; someone would have found her already, but no one did. Then the music stopped, and I looked out and saw you two, and I knew it was real." The young boy begins to tremble as he recalls the events that took the life of the woman. "I was sitting on an old fallen tree at the edge of the woods, throwing rocks at the little woodland animals. Then I heard a commotion near me. I went to see what it was, and there was Thea, struggling with a ... a ... a monster. It had its claws over her mouth; then ... then ... then it ... it took her away into the sky."

The lad stands silent after his testimony, a blank look on his face. Samiah pats him on the shoulder, and then he and Nahmas walk a few steps away from the boy. "He speaks of a monster? What do you think of it, Nahmas?" Samiah asks.

"I believe he speaks of the myth of the Nameless One, a wretched creature that steals the souls of humans. It is folklore, though ... a story aimed to keep people close together. But if what this boy says is true, the Nameless One may be more than a myth. This child may be the only one who has seen it up close and lived to tell about it."

Samiah looks at Nahmas curiously. "I have traveled great distances yet have never heard of this creature of which you speak. Why?"

"The myth of the Nameless One is more common in the lands far past our territories, Samiah."

"Do you believe it to be true, a monster?" Samiah asks his friend apprehensively.

"I believe that boys have big imaginations," Nahmas says firmly.

Samiah thinks about the dead woman they recently discovered, and he thinks about Lebis. "Well, I do not know about a soul-sucking Nameless One, but something strange is happening, Nahmas; could it be a beast, a wild animal of some sort? Maybe it flies; maybe it does not. But if this is what attacked Lebis, how did Eramane get away? Her body would have been discovered as well. She had to have escaped somehow," Samiah states confidently.

Nahmas quickly reminds Samiah of the boy's testimony. "The boy claimed that the creature flew away with the woman. If that is true, then ..."

"Then maybe it took Eramane too? Is that what you are saying?" Samiah shouts. "Took her where? It does not eat its victims. Why would it take her   ?"

"No, it does not eat them; it is believed that it takes their soul."

Samiah gives Nahmas a look of disbelief and turns to speak with the boy. Shouts from the villagers claim Samiah's attention as the angry townspeople run toward him and his comrade. They are screaming foul things at the two men.

"You murdering bastards!" one of the village men yells.

"Both of you shall pay!" shouts another as they approach. Samiah and Nahmas draw their weapons. Samiah stands fierce with his sword pointing straight out. Nahmas plants his feet firmly and aims his bow at the crowd.

"Get back!" Samiah demands.

"You killed my Thea!" the dead girl's mother screams.

"We did not kill her! Stand down now! Ask that boy over there what killed her." Samiah points in the direction of the boy witness. The villagers look over to see nothing; to Samiah's astonishment, the boy is gone. He and Nahmas, both guarded, know they will have to fight the angry mob of distraught villagers.

Silence fills the damp night air as Samiah and Nahmas wait for the angry mob to attack. "Do not kill these men, Nahmas; they are driven by fear and remorse. If we disarm a few of them, we can run for our horses and ride out. On three now … one, two, three!"

They engage to disarm the men. It is not a difficult task to relieve the villagers of their weapons; these people are unskilled farmers, armed with only farming tools, and they have been drinking ale all night. Clumsily fighting, a couple of scruffy drunkards lose their weapons. Samiah and Nahmas bolt to their horses and ride into the woods. The mob follows but stops at the tree line and turns back, knowing that they cannot catch the Riders.

The sun is coming up, painting streaks of bright white across the horizon. It seems like days since the sun has made an appearance, and Samiah wonders if the mighty orb will stay with them all day or be cast over by another intrusion of heavy clouds. His search for Eramane has been unsuccessful, and his hopes for finding her are dwindling. Samiah's face is grim and his heart beats to the tune of sorrow. Nahmas is at his side, riding in silence, looking to the horizon. Samiah has no idea where Eramane could be. Torbiun clansmen, flying beasts …

his concern deepens as he imagines what Eramane might have suffered if she lived through the tragic events that took place at the meadow. He wonders if his sister had to witness the death of her companion, her newfound friend. Mostly he wonders if his sister has already met the same fate as Lebis, her body found by someone who does not know her, who does not love her.

"I do not know what to say to my parents. I dread seeing their faces when I tell them we have not found Eramane." Samiah's words are low, sad. Nahmas does not reply to any of these remarks. He knows he does not have words that will help his friend.

As they continue making their way to Eludwid Hall, Nahmas thinks about the myth of the Nameless One. It is an outlandish idea, but to Nahmas it is a scenario that makes sense; he decides to approach it as if he were planning an attack strategy for Lord Danius. It does not take long for him to come to a useful conclusion.

"We have to rethink this situation, Samiah. Thea's attack resembles the assault on Lebis, yes?"

"Yes."

"And the boy from Thea's village said that it had wings … that it could fly?" Again Nahmas looks to Samiah for confirmation.

"Yes, the boy mentioned wings."

"If Lebis and Thea were attacked by the Nameless One, could you imagine that they would look other than they did?" Nahmas questions, pointing out the minimal wounds on both bodies.

"I do not know what a person should look like if they were relieved of their soul, but they could resemble Lebis's and Thea's remains, I suppose," Samiah confirms. "Are you truly trying to convince me that we are looking for a creature that flies and"—he searches for fitting words—"harvests our souls? It sounds absurd!"

"I agree. It does sound as if we are mad. But as absurd as it seems, it is the only explanation that makes sense of all this. We just interrogated the Torbiuns and detained them; they do not have Eramane, and we both know that. Ulic had no idea what you were speaking of. Samiah, we have seen many things on our journeys that other men have not; I was saved by a man who can summon fire with a thought. If that type of power exists without question, a flying beast is but child's play." Samiah remains silent. "Why should we ignore this possibility?" Nahmas urges.

"Based on the testimony of a child, you mean?"

"That, and the point that we know it was not the Torbiuns." Nahmas hesitates, understanding that he needs to reach Samiah another way. "Samiah, you are like my brother; Eramane is dear to us as well. Your pain is not unfelt by your brothers. If I did not think that what I am suggesting made sense, we would not be discussing it at all. Animals do not waste their kill, but the Nameless One would have no use for the bodies."

Samiah gives in, feeling that it might well be their only other option, his last hope. "Fine, Nahmas, let us explore this. So the attack on Lebis and the attack on Thea were about a three days' ride apart."

"That means it has a large hunting territory," Nahmas says in disappointment.

"It also means that it is a large creature."

"It does."

"Which means ..." Samiah stops to let Nahmas finish the thought.

"Which means something that size can live in only so many places."

Samiah has a new hope that he will find his sister. He gives a command to his steed, and he and Nahmas make haste back toward Eludwid.

CHAPTER FOURTEEN

DISHEARTENING NEWS

THE SKY IS A DARK, starless abyss. Through the night Samiah and Nahmas ride, until they finally reach Eludwid Hall; darkness still cloaks them as they gallop through the streets of Eludwid. Their steeds slow to a trot as they approach the Hall. Several horses are tied to posts; they swish their tails and snort the cold out of their noses; one hangs its head, resting. The Riders dismount and walk their horses over to the posts to hitch them as well. Samiah gives his horse a pat and walks up the stairs to the Hall. Nahmas follows seconds later, after thanking his own steed for its services, as the Ghosts always do.

Lord Danius's chamber looks the same as it did when Samiah was last there. Piles of paper lie about, books are stacked one on the other along the walls, and scrolls poke out of leather sacks by the hundreds. The chamber feels welcom-

ing despite the clutter, and a firm hug from his burly lord
brings Samiah a comfort much needed.

"You Riders handled the Torbiuns well, as I expected. But
that expression on your face is unmistakable, Samiah; you
could not hide it from me if you tried." Lord Danius pulls
out his chair and motions for Samiah to sit. Samiah hesitates,
never having been offered a seat in Lord Danius's chair. "Come
on now, sit. Tell me what is on that brain of yours."

"I discovered a young woman's corpse not far from the
Torbiuns' camp. Nahmas and I investigated it while the other
Riders were sent back here. We rode into Mountains End,
where we learned that a boy witnessed her death." Samiah
pauses, not knowing how to explain what he and Nahmas
have concluded.

"Well?" Lord Danius urges.

"The witness claims that a beast flew off with the woman."
Samiah searches Lord Danius's face for approval, disbelief, anything. Their ruler does no more than sniff, indicating to Samiah
that he needs to continue. Samiah explains the proposal he
and Nahmas put together, clarifying how they concluded the
possible whereabouts of the creature called the Nameless One.
"This is our best chance at finding her," Samiah finishes.

Lord Danius stands quiet for a moment, looking out of
the tower's only window. He turns to his Riders.

"Earlier today I was looking through that very window,
and I watched the townsfolk below; they all seemed to be
rushing to their destinations. Not a single one had a leisurely
stride, and not a single one was single; they were herded, be-
having the way animals do in the wild," Lord Danius says.

"Do you know what this means?" Samiah and the brothers remain silent.

"It means my people are afraid, Samiah. Word of the blacksmith's death and your sister's disappearance has struck fear in every resident of Eludwid," Lord Danius relates. "I was sure the capture of the Torbiuns would bring relief to them, but I fear that a more sinister threat burdens them." The lord turns to his Riders. "A beast? With wings?" Lord Danius pauses for a moment, thinking about what Samiah has suggested. "Well, I cannot say that it does not sound farfetched, but if you think this will be the answer to finding your sister, then I will do what I can to help you."

"My Lord, I will need all the men you can spare," Samiah says. "Riders, footmen, watermen, all you can spare."

"That can be arranged. Take leave for the night; see your families. I will have the orders drawn." Lord Danius dips a quill and writes up the orders, handing them to a guard just outside the chamber door. "There, the men will be ready morning after next."

"Thank you, Lord Danius," Samiah says.

"I would like to accompany you to your parents' home. I want to be there when you explain the ordeal; they may have an easier time believing all of this if I am there with you." Samiah knows that the ruler wishes to accompany him only because he is restless, and a visit outside of the town will help him feel useful.

"My parents would like that very much," Samiah says and follows Lord Danius out of the chamber.

Samiah and his company reach his parents' home, and as he approaches the main house, he looks out to the stables and signals to one of the caretaker's children. From the distance he cannot determine which one it is, but he waves them over anyway. The child runs over and Samiah is relieved it is one of the older children, able to ride a message to Mira.

"Send message to my wife that I am here," Samiah requests.

"Yes, sir," the boy says, darting off to the stables in excitement. He is no doubt pleased with his errand; an excuse to ride out beyond the fields is worthy of the fuss.

Samiah hangs his head in shame as he enters the sitting area where his parents wait. Before he opens the door, he hears his mother's voice. She sounds as though she has been crying. Her whimper of a voice is deafening to Samiah. He sighs heavily and enters into the room.

"Samiah, my son, have you found her?" Alora Fahnestock asks with hope as she stands from the chair. She clutches her handkerchief, awaiting an answer. Randall Fahnestock stands next to the fireplace, with the same look as his wife's. Samiah can only shake his head no in response. Alora loses her ability to stand and turns her head to search for her chair. She throws herself into the leather chair and lets out moaning cries for her daughter. Randall walks up to Samiah and hugs him.

"I am glad you made it home safe, my son," he says, as he tries to comfort Samiah.

"Has she been like this the whole time?" Samiah asks, staring at his distraught mother.

"She has not been able to staunch the tears since we heard
the news." Randall tries to summon strength, but his throat
knots up when he speaks.

Lord Danius stays behind on the porch for a moment,
long enough to give Samiah time to break the disappointing
news; the Ghosts wait with him. It is not long before Samiah
steps out and invites them in.

Even with Lord Danius at his side, Samiah finds it difficult
to explain to his parents what he believes may have happened
to Eramane. He watches his mother's face form an expression
of terror as "winged beast" leaves his mouth. His father listens
closely, hanging on to every detail. While Samiah speaks with
his parents, the Fahnestocks' caretakers prepare meals for the
exhausted Riders and their lord.

Mira arrives just before they sit to eat. Samiah grabs her
up in his arms and buries his face in her hair. "Oh, how I have
missed you," he says.

"I have missed you too, love," she says softly. Samiah sets
her down and places his hand on her belly.

"How are you feeling?"

"Some days are worse than others, but for now, I feel
great!" She takes Samiah's face in her hands. "Eramane?" she
asks.

"We have an idea of some places she might be," he says,
and again finds himself explaining his outrageous notion.
Mira's face mirrors his mother's, and it makes Samiah doubt

himself. But Mira knows her husband and sees that her reaction is affecting him.

"If I were the one in her place, I would find comfort in knowing that you were the one looking for me," Mira says, and Samiah's self-doubt fades a bit. "I am starving, so let's eat," she adds after catching the smells from the galley.

Each of them eats, but the process is forced, and if not for Lord Danius's stories from his childhood to lighten the atmosphere, the meal would have transpired in silence. Samiah is grateful for Lord Danius's anecdotes. Alora Fahnestock decides to help Oriana clean up, in hopes that the task will divert her thoughts.

At last the power of exhaustion takes hold of Samiah and the Ghosts; they each take to a room rest for several hours; on the road, sleep will not come so easily. Samiah and Mira lie in his bed, the bed he slept in when he still lived with his parents. He thinks about his pregnant wife and how he wishes he could be at her side every moment. Unable to take advantage of sleep, Samiah goes through the strategy of their hunt while he stares up at the ceiling, his wife asleep in his arms. Their plan is to search any caves they encounter and canvass the most remote mountain ranges. Since they believe the beast they are searching for to be two or three times larger than a man, it seems obvious that it would need a large, secluded place to live. Samiah hopes that they are following the right path; it is all the hope that he has in finding his sister.

Morning dawns and Lord Danius suggests that they recruit
Eludwid's allies to the north, the Vegamonians, to aid Samiah.
They know of the most remote places in those lands and ev-
erything in between.

"Give this to a messenger Rider in town. Have him ride
north and give it to Roshamar," Lord Danius commands
Aurick, and he and Terrin swiftly leave the Fahnestocks' home
in search of a messenger Rider. "Riders will be ready by morning at the Hall. I will ride back with you then. I should probably get back to my duties sooner, but it is so quiet out here;
sometimes a man needs the quiet," Lord Danius says, taking a
seat on the porch.

The day has come and gone. Samiah escorted his wife back
home and has just returned from the short trip. He notices
the horses are alarmed as he hitches his steed to the post, and
wonders why they have not been put up in the stables for the
night. Nahmas notices Samiah's arrival and walks out to greet
his comrade.

"I took Lord Danius to view your property this afternoon.
We arrived back a short time ago," Nahmas says, noticing
Samiah's curiosity about the unattended horses.

"They are jumpy, on edge since Mountains End," Samiah
says.

"Yes. They have been on edge for a few days now," Nahmas
declares, moving down to calm his stallion. The two men continue to stroke the disturbed horses. Nahmas clears off mist

that has settled on the back of his horse. He quietly inspects his steed, making sure it has no injuries from their last ride. He picks up each hoof and looks it over. Satisfied, Nahmas turns his attention from the snorting animal and thinks of Samiah. He wonders what will happen to his comrade if Eramane is never found. What will the guilt do to Samiah, and will he ever forgive himself?

CHAPTER FIFTEEN

THE SYCOPHANT

MOST OF THE GRAND PALACE displays rare beauties; other parts are not so grand. Its bowels are the vicinity where rare beauty cannot be found. Adikiah's servants live there. There is nothing spectacular to observe. Servants walk around as if they are trudging through mud, not having anything to do but wait for Adikiah's command. These faceless creatures have become Adikiah's servants by obsession. They long to be like him but cannot. They have nothing to offer the Orders of the Reach that tend the other side of the Gate.

Down in a dark corridor, one of Adikiah's servants decides that it can wile Adikiah into believing that his chosen companion will never accept her new life, that she will never truly belong to him, never want to be with him. This maniacal servant envies Eramane, and it wants her cast out of the palace.

"She is not worthy of her new gift," a tall, dark figure speaks to itself in a deep, raspy voice that sounds like something has a tight grip around its throat. "Her soul was too pure. It is not possible that she surrendered it entirely," the servant finishes. It paces up and down the unlit hall, ranting to itself, waiting for the opportunity to engage its master.

CHAPTER SIXTEEN

Vague Memories

THE WIND BLOWS GENTLY ENOUGH, yet a soft whisper of misery hangs on it, like a ripe apple not wanting to fall from the branch. I wake from a deep slumber; surprisingly sleep comes easily. I lie on the floor of the landing, reflecting on the events that almost killed me; I grimace. It angers me to know that I was almost killed by frozen water and gigantic splinters. I am completely healed, and while my mind fights against my actions, I cannot force myself to starve again. My second harvest sparked a flame, and it burns with fury, fueling an instinct that lies within me. But the flow of primal survival coursing through me never fully coats the guilt. I am remorseful that I killed those people, and as I recollect the harvests, I return to the same conclusion each time: Adikiah will always find a way to coerce me. *Adikiah. Adikiah—where is he?*

I look around the terrace for my creator. This is the first time I have not been able to sense him since I *became*. I fly down to his terrace. Not seeing him, I make my way into the mountain. I have been in here only once since my becoming, to wash after the attack that almost killed me. I do not like being inside of the mountain palace, but my curiosity drives me deep down into its belly. I search each room, with no success. Where could he be? I enter the eating chamber, the room with the amber columns and grand chandelier. As I enter, I feel as though I am walking in it for the first time. The embellishments remain as they were, but my eyes see them differently. Glittering gems look like thousands of tiny explosions; I hear wax splash on the floor as it drips from the burning candles. The columns next to the hearth, once appearing as softly glowing amber, now look like flaming tridents.

"To what do I owe the pleasure?" Adikiah is behind me. "I thought you would never again enter this place," he says.

"I was looking for you," I say.

"You found me."

His answer irritates me.

"Would you like to eat?" he asks. "Food," he adds.

I almost reject his offer, but the thought of eating entices me; it is something I can do to make me feel human again.

"I would not mind to eat," I say. And just as I remember, Adikiah motions and servants fill the table with food. It does not look the same as it used to either. The meats look a drab grayish color, and they smell repugnant. The bread smells sour and the cheeses even more so, like spoiled cream left in a hot stable all day. I look around for anything that I can manage to put in my mouth. I notice a bowl of berries; they smell sweet. I take one from the bowl and hold it up, examining its color, bright red, like the setting sun. I put it in my mouth and squeeze it until it squirts its sugary juices all over my tongue. The berry tastes like sweet longing, and I, in this small moment, am elated. I roll it in my mouth, savoring its sweet taste, and then images flash before me: a blanket strewn with food, sunbeams darting through tall trees, blue eyes—a soft kiss on my forehead! I shove my chair back and storm out of the eating chamber. I feel like I cannot breathe; I need the fresh air I can get only form the landing, and that is where I am headed.

I must have snatched the bowl of berries from the table before I hurried out; I hold them as I stare out at the ocean. The winds from the ocean are strong this evening, and I watch as the water churns in synchronization with the high winds.

"A storm is coming," I say, hearing Adikiah land. He maintains his true form.

"We must harvest again; we will go tonight," he says.

"We harvested only days ago," I say.

"A few days are the extent of a soul's sustenance," he says plainly. I say nothing, only look out to the ocean. My attention comes back to the landing as I realize that Adikiah has summoned a servant up here. "Tell her what you told me, slave," Adikiah orders the sycophant. The frail being looks frightened but holds its ground with its master.

"She is not worthy of your gifts, my master. You should have chosen me to bestow immortality upon," its grudging voice replies. Adikiah looks to me, examining my reaction. The servant continues, "She is unfit and carries intensions within that are false, my master."

I am not threatened by what the servant has said. Instead I feel pity for it. The life of a servant from the Reach must be even more burdensome than mine.

"We are the same, you and I," I say to the shadow skeleton that sways back and forth, fearing that it has crossed a boundary with its master. "We were both forced into a life that we would not have chosen for ourselves." The servant looks up at me, and I see that it has a face; *she* has a face. It is not detailed, but basic structures are in place: eyes, nose, and mouth. Her skin is opaque and looks like parchment, but her dark gray coloring and elongated features testify to her origins of the Reach, the only place I can imagine that creatures like her would come from. Her black eyes are set deep in their sockets, explaining why I was never able to see them before, as the servants most always keep their heads bowed.

"You see, master, she does not appreciate her new gift," the servant rasps out.

"I want her to leave," I say calmly. The servant does not move; she most likely awaits orders from her master. "Leave!" I shout. This time the reluctant servant obeys me and leaps from the landing, the only way to get back into the palace.

"You are staying up here until we leave, I assume," Adikiah says.

"Yes," I snap. When my reply comes out so harsh and full, it makes me wonder how much longer Adikiah will accept my rebellion. His feelings for me must be fading after the abhorrence I have shown him over the past few weeks. Adikiah turns to leave.

"Wait!" He halts and turns to me.

"What is it?"

"My memories are returning," I say to him.

"What are they?" he asks, concern in his voice.

"I think they are of a young man and me, having a picnic in the forest."

"Anything else?" he pries.

"No," I say, wishing it were a lie.

"Did I not tell you they would return?"

"Yes, you did, Adikiah."

"Soon you will have all of them, Eramane," he says, turning again to leave.

"Adikiah." He stops for me again. "Why do you possess one of your kind in the relic chamber?" He sighs. He had not expected that I would remember the relic chamber above memories of my family.

"He was my creator."

"How did he die?" I ask.

"I took his life, Eramane."

"Why?"

He flexes his wings, and they spread out to their fullest width.

"Because he betrayed me," he answers, then dives from the landing. *Because he betrayed me* revolves in my mind until I replace it with those precious, vague memories of a picnic in the forest.

CHAPTER SEVENTEEN

A GREAT LOSS

It is time FOR OUR next harvest. Adikiah tells me that the town we are harvesting from is a long distance from the mountain palace.

"You will need to keep up; fly with haste. We must make it back to the mountain before dawn or risk being spotted in the air."

As we stand on the landing, I look over to Adikiah. He reaches for my hand; it is a risky gesture, but I allow him to take it, unsure why I do. His hand clasps mine and my earlier thoughts on his feelings for me are answered; they have not lessened, yet they are tainted with jealousy, of what I do not know. He pulls my hand to his lips and kisses it. "Let us not find the same trouble as we did the last time," he says and releases his grip. He spreads his leathery wings and takes to the night sky; time to see how well I can keep up.

We are in flight for several hours before we reach the homes Adikiah has chosen. We circle above a stone house backed by trees. Smoke rises from the chimney, and several horses are hitched out front; they must have sensed our presence, because they are stamping at the ground.

"There are three inside, Eramane," he says, yet I already know, for I too can see their hearts beating. I look down at two men tending horses; their hearts beat strong, and I wonder why we are here, targeting a group of five humans, when all we need are two. But we are too close now; if I ask Adikiah, the men below are sure to hear.

We decide to enter through the back of the home. Adikiah sets down first, and I am directly behind. I look at the entry. "You will not fit through that," I say. Adikiah sees my point.

"Keep going; I will meet you there," he says and flies off. I continue stalking my way through the house. The back rooms are unlit, but to me it looks as if day fills them. I walk by a room whose door is open. Inside are a bed, a long mirror, and a rack filled with dresses. I pass it and take in the smell of the home; they have eaten recently. Finally I approach the room where three people, three souls, unknowingly await their deaths. I peek through a small crack between the wall boards; they cannot see me, but each of them is in my sights. One is an older man wearing an elaborate robe. He is a ruler, no doubt, and his age will make for an easy harvest. Another of the victims is a beautiful middle-aged woman, and the third a stout man, likely to be the woman's husband. I watch the humans, and for a moment I feel a familiarity with these people. I listen to the woman, her voice sad and distraught. I wonder what has taken happiness from her.

I am rattled when Adikiah erupts through the front entry-way, spilling into the room where the lady with the sad voice stares in horror. Their eyes fall on him, and like frightened rabbits, they freeze. The woman screams out, and Adikiah looks for me. He spots me, peering out from behind the wall. "Take her!" he orders. I hurry over to her while she continues to scream, frozen in fear. I hoist her in the air by her neck. Her vocal cords strain under my grip.

Knocking the middle-aged man to the floor, Adikiah moves swiftly and clasps his Goliath hands around the neck of the elder, placing his other hand on the nobleman's head. I hear the woman gasping for air, and I focus my attention back to her. Our eyes lock and I am momentarily confused. She is familiar, and that stays me from harvesting. "Eramane?" she chokes out. I hear commotion from the disheveled man on the floor; he grabs at his chest. The man cannot take in air. Adikiah, finished with his first harvest, looks over at the breathless man and sees him clutching his chest. But his approach is halted when the two men from outside enter the room.

Adikiah yells to me, "Eramane! Harvest from her!" I face this woman again, and for the second time, I cannot kill her. The two men who recently joined us stand for a moment in disbelief. One has a bow and sends an arrow at Adikiah; it hardly pricks his flesh. The other looks at the woman squirming beneath my grasp.

"Mother!" he cries out and runs at me, drawing his weapon. As he charges, he slips on water that has been spilled on the floor during the discord. The man's momentum causes him to crash to the floor and slide across, stopping underneath a table. Adikiah grabs his attacker by the face and tosses him across the room, sending him into a bookcase. I drop the woman, the woman who spoke my name. Everyone's actions slow, as if we are underwater, and I scan the room, taking in all of the violence: the corpse of the ruler, the dying man writhing on the floor, the sad woman coughing as she takes in air, the fallen man under the table.

"Eramane, kill him now!" Adikiah commands. I reach down for the man underneath the table, but then the helpless warrior speaks.

"Eramane?" he asks, searching my face. As soon as my name escapes his lips I know who he is, I know who the coughing woman is, the dying man, and the dead nobleman.

"Samiah," I swallow, and just as Adikiah promised, all of my memories come flooding back to me, like the churning ocean waters that hurl themselves at the mountain base, all in that that moment. I am mortified that I nearly killed my mother.

"Kill him!" Adikiah screams. "Kill him now, Eramane!" Adikiah screams his order again.

"No! No, I cannot!" I reply tearfully. Memories of my life, of the meadow, and of Adikiah hammer away at me; the room begins to spin. *May the gods forgive me.* Hopelessness envelops me; I cannot breathe. As if my life were choked out of me, I faint.

"No!" Adikiah shouts and picks me up into his arms. He makes no effort to be graceful in my home and smashes through anything in his way until he reaches the exit. Adikiah and I are in the air in seconds and heading to his mountain.

CHAPTER EIGHTEEN

SAMIAH'S NEW COMMAND

SAMIAH STAYS ON THE FLOOR by his father's side. It takes a few moments before the older man passes; fright from laying eyes on Adikiah brought an end to him. Nahmas staggers over to Alora and helps her to her feet. Samiah holds his father tightly and sobs as Nahmas helps Alora over to her dead husband.

"I am sorry, my friend. Your loss is great, but we can do nothing for them here," Nahmas says. Samiah does not want to leave his father and Lord Danius lying on the floor of the house. The father of the caretaker family rushes in with a long, sharp plowing tool in his hand.

"What happened here? I heard the screams and rushed over," he says, searching the wreckage. "Oh no!" he whimpers, seeing that Randall lies dead in Samiah's arms.

"I have no time to explain; I must find my sister," Samiah says. "Will you see that they are properly buried? And take care of my mother?" He wipes tears from his face.

"Yes, sir," the caretaker replies. Samiah embraces his mother, squeezing her tight.

"I will find her, Mother, and I will bring her back to us," he declares and rushes from the home. "Nahmas, let us ride!"

"Yes, Lord Fahnestock," Nahmas assents. Samiah looks at Nahmas in question.

"What did you say?" Samiah asks.

"Lord Danius is dead. You are his successor." It takes Samiah a moment to piece it together, but Nahmas is correct; the High Commander takes the chair in the eastern tower of Eludwid Hall when its current ruler dies. Samiah's uncle, his mother's brother, would have been the next in line had he not been killed. Now Samiah will succeed Lord Danius. Samiah knows that he now has the power to summon the help of any region he chooses.

"I did not recognize her at first, the red hair," Samiah recollects his sister's altered appearance. "And she was so strong, hoisting Mother up like that. But then the beast called to her; she is a Nameless One too. He made her that way. He took her to be his mate!" Samiah's anger rises. "That is why we could not find her body. That is why he killed Lebis!" His ranting calms. "We have to find them, and kill him," Samiah says solemnly.

"Your sister?" Nahmas asks.

"You saw her—she could not kill our mother. Eramane is fighting. We can save her, but we must hurry," Samiah boasts.

"She is like him, my lord; she may never be the same again," Nahmas suggests.

"She will be as she once was. She is my sister. I cannot abandon her!"

Samiah yanks at the leather girth on the saddle, as Aurick and Terrin crest the hill and gallop down to meet with Samiah and Nahmas.

"Eramane is alive, " Nahmas explains. "She was taken by the Nameless One and changed. They came here tonight and killed Lord Danius and Samiah's father. They would have killed us, but Eramane recognized her brother and backed down."

Aurick and Terrin have news of their own. "We saw the creature above the trees a short time ago. They are traveling east," Terrin says.

Samiah is revived by this news. They are planning to head east anyway. Now Samiah is confident he will find his sister.

"But the shores stretch so far; we may never find them," Aurick notes.

"There are only so many rocks big enough to hide them," Samiah says as he directs his steed to head east. "Well," he says, looking at the Ghosts, "what are we waiting for?" The four set off toward Lunlitch, a city to the east. Samiah thinks of his sister and the tragedy of what has become of her. If he does not get Eramane back now, he may lose her to the Nameless One forever.

CHAPTER NINETEEN

Adikiah's Fury

"WHAT HAVE YOU DONE? YOU have betrayed me, Eramane!"

Adikiah throws me to the stone floor of the landing. His anger is incomprehensible; it flushes itself out through his eyes, suffocating their color, leaving them black. The winds blow rampantly, and I am not on the ground long before Adikiah grabs me up again. I try with all my strength to pry away his claws, but Adikiah has just harvested and is too powerful; I cannot contest with him. His movements are wild and unpredictable; I have never seen him like this before. When our flesh meets, I can hear his thoughts, feel his anger. I see a partial memory of the night he killed his creator. Adikiah's demeanor was much like it is now, and his creator was defenseless, as I am now. Short fragments flow through me, and then, there it is, the moment he murdered his creator; Adikiah plunged his mighty talons into his creator's chest, dislodging a red, pulsing, orblike object. In a way, his rage satisfies me, because now he can feel in this one moment what I have been feeling since that day in the meadow.

Adikiah's wings flap uncontrollably, cutting me with their sharp edges. "I love you! I made you my queen, and you chose your miserable human family over me!" He swoops me down to the terrace and pins me against a stone column, taking my face in his large hands. Again I try to push him away, but it is pointless. I would have stood a chance had I harvested too, but like this I am too weak.

"You took me there to see whom I would choose?" I ask softly. "You did not think that I might remember them?"

He presses his chest against me. "I wanted you to remember them," he huffs. "I wanted you to remember your human family and still choose me!" he roars.

"Please! I could not control it!" I plead. If I do not get through to him, he will end me. My pleas are not consoling, and the more I speak, the more he rages. But to my relief, Adikiah's attention suddenly falls from me.

A black dust appears in the winds that strongly blow around us. It is thin in the beginning and then grows thicker. Adikiah releases me and I collapse. "Leave now, Nulyk. Your presence is not welcome," Adikiah commands. The black dust cloud forms into the being that collected my blood when I *became*. Its distorted face busies itself by changing from one demonic visage to another. A wicked sight I recall too vividly. Nulyk laughs a low, crickety laugh, and tosses an empty canister to the floor.

"They want more," Nulyk says.

"What more can I give them?" Adikiah asks. His chest heaves with every breath, and his wings flex.

"You have made a mistake, mighty one. Did you really think you could possess such purity all for yourself?" Nulyk laughs as its body begins to churn. "She will be your demise," it says. The burdensome creature contorts into a whirlwind and heads back to the sky; it glances back at us. "They want her," it reveals before disappearing into the night sky. I lose my desire to fight, and unconscious I am left to Adikiah's mercy.

CHAPTER TWENTY

THE GATE

"I WILL WAIT A THOUSAND YEARS for you, Era-mane." It sounds like a whisper in a dream, yet when I open my eyes and look around the chamber, I see that I am no longer dreaming. I also see a wall that looks as if water reflects on it ... and that sound, what is that sound? Like the hum of a blade when it has been struck by another. Only this vibratory noise resonates within the mountain walls, and it draws out in an offensive note that strikes the ear in a maddening way. Although I have not been in this chamber, I know where I am: the Gate chamber, the chamber where Adikiah transports souls to the Orders of the Reach. He once briefly mentioned this room to me but has never brought me here, not until now. I hear the trickle of water dripping from the walls. I try to move, but I cannot; my limbs are numb, and a familiar sweet taste lingers in my mouth. "I cannot risk you bringing down my mountain," Adikiah had said, forcing the liquid in my mouth before leaving the terrace.

Adikiah approaches me and kneels down to the floor. He has calmed since our last encounter on the terrace. His face is level with mine, and he is not in his true form; he is the beautiful man that disguises his fiendish image. In the few seconds before he speaks again, I wonder many things. I wonder if death is still capable of bringing me peace. I wonder about my family. Did Adikiah kill my brother and mother before taking me back to the palace? I pray that they are still alive, because I have every intention of surviving Adikiah's wrath and making him pay for what he has done to my family.

My seconds of thought cease with Adikiah's voice. "I was wrong to have trusted a human, but your powers over me are strong," he says. "Now I must keep you down here until your will is broken, until you grow to love me, until you accept your new life, or until that noise drives you out." I thought that I had despised him before; my feelings run far deeper than that now. I should have tried to end him after my second harvest, when I was stronger. Adikiah was wise to sedate me; if I had the chance now, I would die trying to defeat him.

"If it takes a thousand years, Eramane, I will wait," he says, rising to his feet. An abrupt feeling of amusement stirs within me, as I realize I am beginning to feel my body. Did Adikiah not get enough down my throat? Was the concoction not strong enough? Either way I can move, and Adikiah is in his human form!

Adikiah turns from me and makes his way to the chamber door. I do not hesitate; pushing off from the floor, I lunge at him. I hit him and the impact sends us into the door, my arms around his throat. I lock him up tight and squeeze; he thrashes about, trying to shake me, a futile attempt. We fall to the ground and the impact separates us, giving Adikiah the opportunity he needs to transform. Hope escapes me as I watch his instantaneous change; now his power trumps mine. I turn and run to the end of the chamber, putting distance between us. I cannot let this be the end. I have been through too much; my family has suffered too greatly. He does not deserve this victory; I do! My body begins to tingle, and my flesh tightens, as though I have jumped into freezing water. I stare at Adikiah as he rushes toward me, and as I focus on him, I notice that his flesh has begun to split and tear away from his body, a detail that has not escaped his attention. He howls in pain as his skin breaks and cracks, though he does not cease his advance. Adikiah pummels me and sends me against the wall; he steps back immediately, eyes wide. I stick to it, like a meaningless bug in a spider's web. Looking at me with such sorrow and astonishment, he cries out to the wall, "You cannot have her!" My body begins to penetrate the wall, as the hard, rocky surface gives way to a penetrable mass. I struggle to free myself and feel something grabbing at me. At first I do not know what it is, but after a moment I can tell it is a set of hands trying to pull me into the rock. Lanky, grayish-black arms reach out from the wall, holding me, wrapping around my body. I scream in frustration and confusion. Then they begin to cut me and stab me with their long nails. I wail as I beg Adikiah to help me. "Please! Kill me! Do not let them take me!"

"No!" Adikiah screams as he tries to free me from the wall. "No! I am sorry my love!" Adikiah pleads as he tries with all of

his might to free me from the arms of the Gate. "Let her go!"
he yells. It is too late. As the last part of my body disappears
into the wall, he grabs my hand and then has to let it go. He
howls his objection, and his screams fill the palace.

The arms that pulled me into the Gate have abandoned me,
and I peer around the quiet tunnel, standing motionless. I do
not know where I am, only that this place is haunting, unforgiving. Subtle moans fill the tunnel, and my head. The moans
sound like starving vagrants in the streets, begging with their
last efforts for compassion. As I make my way down the dark,
foggy passage, the moans grow louder. Soaked with my own
blood, I shiver in the cold, dank air. The arms that pulled me
in tore at me viciously. I shiver more violently as the sounds
from within become intolerable. Near the end of the short
passage I see an opening into a vast, murky area. I enter the
dense vicinity, and the sounds become words. "Eramane," they
call. Something whips past me, hitting my shoulder, nearly
knocking me to my knees. "Eramane," again they call. A vine-
like object wraps around my ankle. "Come pay for your sins,"
they chant as the restraint pulls me to the ground and carries
me to my atonement.

Thousands of souls shriek at me as they have their way with
my body. Ripping skin from my back and legs, they thrash at

me. At times, only one or two will attack me, and other times they all join in. I scream for death to come and take me, but my words are masked by the souls who mock me louder than I can cry out. They laugh at my pain; it riles them. The more I cry, the more they tear at my flesh. The pain of *becoming* is no contest to the misery these souls are causing. On my back, I feel an intense pressure, like the weight of something tugging at my arm; only the tug is forceful and delivered with fervor. I realize what it is just as the pressure turns to pain; a soul has latched on to one of my wings, and it intends on tearing it from me. I cannot stop it, there are too many, and guarding my face is more important. But the pain increases, and at its peak I hear the ripping noise from behind me. My hands move from my face despite myself and search my shoulder, finding only a raw hole where the wing was attached. The soul carries my wing off like a trophy; "Look what I have done to her," it seems to boast. My ordeal is far from over, for I have another wing, and an envious soul has witnessed the delight in possessing one of them. In one swift motion, a soul latches onto my wing, twisting and pulling until at last it has secured its own declaration.

I want to give up. I offer myself to death and await release from the pain, but death does not come for me. What does come is a familiar face; it appears at my side. "Father?" I look at the figure, trying to gain a better focus. It *is* my father.. "Father, why are you here?"

I begin to panic; the thought of my father being harvested disturbs me beyond measure. My father does not belong here. He leans close to me and says, "I am not here, Eramane."

He places his forefinger on my heart. "I am *here*, my child. You must survive this; your mother and brother need you. We need you." His soft whisper comforts me as he strokes my bloody hair. "Use your gift; you are very powerful. I love you, my child," he says, kissing my forehead, and then vanishes into the nothingness.

Can I summon the power to escape this madness? Do I really have the strength to force these atrocities off me? Adikiah told me I had a gift too. I recall forcing the crack to widen; I remember Adikiah's flesh cracking across its surface. Did I do that? I close my eyes and take in the pain. I tense my body and focus; my surroundings begin to quake, and the air ripples like water when a stone has been thrown into it. The ground or my body—I cannot differentiate—begins to tremble, and one at a time the souls cease their assaults on me. More violently the ground shakes, and then, in a swift exhalation, the souls flee from me.

Silence; there is no more shrieking and wailing—no more pain. Here I stand in the passage, alone. How do I get out of here? There must be a way. In all directions, there is only murky vastness. I have no choice but to walk until I find a way out, and that is what I do—walk. Hours pass, or eternity—who knows? I have not seen or heard anything; nothing accompanies me here. There are no doors. Doors … doors … then it occurs to me—doors! Adikiah can open the Gate; maybe I can too! I imagine myself exiting the Gate, freeing myself from this purgatory. I stare out into the black, and my vision tunnels, forming a soft white hole in front of me, and just that easily, I am sent soaring down the passage. Unfortunately, I did not take into account where the Gate would open, only that I wanted it to open, and I realize that I am falling from the heavens above. I close my eyes just before hitting the ground; it is not going to feel good.

The rain falls to the earth relentlessly. I lie motionless on the ground. My mouth is full of mud, for I cannot lift my head. Maybe I will die tonight. My body suffers greatly from wounds inflicted in the Gate. I feel immense pain, which is welcoming, since I have caused much pain for others. My face burns, and I am sure the gashes on my body are taking in as much mud as my mouth is. All I can taste is blood and wet earth. I am covered in my own fluids, gashed worse than a warrior who fought an entire army by himself and lost. My body trembles from the forceful impact of hitting the ground, and I know that I do not deserve to live.

CHAPTER TWENTY-ONE

"It Is She!"

DESPITE THE NOISE FROM THE torrential rains, I can hear what sounds like an old boat hitting the rocks at the bottom of an ocean cliff. Past the sound comes the smell. It is the luring sweet smell of humans. I know they have to be near, for they smell strongly, even with mud in my nostrils. I hear the hard breathing, the sure sound of tired livestock; it is likely to be several horses pulling a cart. The source of the noise is drawing near. In the dark, with all the rain, the horses might trample me. Then I hear a voice.

"Whoa!" The driver of the wagon shouts to the horses. "There is someone in the road," he yells. "I think it is her!" Another man steps down from the wagon, sinking ankle-deep into the mud. He approaches my defenseless body, leans down, and starts to roll me onto my back. The pain is agonizing, and I scream out, hoping he will cease moving my mutilated body. Then the man leans in close to get a good look at me. He is old, with long gray hair. His face is wrinkled and worn, and he has only one eye. The socket where his other eye should be is just skin and scars. "It is she!" He yells back to the man in the carriage, shouting above the rain. "Limearsy, I cannot lift her. You must get her onto the wagon. She will die if we do not hurry!"

The wagon driver jumps down off the wagon and lifts me from the mud. I cannot see him very well because of the muck that was forced into every orifice of my face, but I can tell he is strong, and if he were not helping me, then he would have been the one to end my life, out here, alone in the dark. The brawny Limearsy places me on the wagon, and the old, one-eyed man yells again above the rain, "We must give her the elixir!"

"I will give it to her, Derkumon," says Limearsy, taking a small leather pouch from the one-eyed man. The young man holds my head up and pours a loathsome concoction down my throat. It is hot and bitter and not something I have ever tasted before. It has to be a healing mix, because even if someone wished to end their life, they would not drink this.

"It is down; let us be on our way," orders Limearsy, and the old man grabs the reins, commanding the horses to move. Soon after I consume the bitter drink, I lose consciousness and leave my fate in the hands of the strangers.

Lightning cracks, waking me, and we pull up to a stone cottage surrounded by trees. Limearsy gently lifts me into his arms and carries me inside the stone house, into a room lit with a few candles. A stumpy woman with frazzled tufts of hair falling out of their pins scurries past Limearsy and turns down blankets so he can put me to bed.

"Oh, the poor child," the housemaid exclaims, and they begin to look over the wounds on my body.

"What happened to you?" Limearsy asks, as though he expects me, lying almost dead, to answer him. Though I hear his words, I cannot respond to them. All I can do is remain at the mercy of these people.

"Who on earth could survive such an attack?" the woman asks herself before leaving the room for a washing vase.

Derkumon bursts into the room, his long, tawny cloak flowing behind him. "Derkumon, she needs more medicine; she suffers greatly," Limearsy exclaims with concern. His concern seems peculiar. Why would a stranger feel concern for me? I am a horrible being, and it seems as if they know yet are undaunted by that. The housemaid returns with a washing vase and sets the warm water next to the bedside. She pulls up a stool and begins cleaning my gashes. The cloth soaks in my blood and colors the basin water red after its first rinse.

"I will have to change this a hundred times before she is properly cleaned," she says.

"Let us go, my son. Maladine will clean her up and give her some more of your elixir," says Derkumon, noticing Limearsy's concern. "I am sure she will pull through, my son. She has made it this far; she will be all right," Derkumon finishes. The old man grabs Limearsy's hand and pats it as if to comfort him. He puts his hand on Limearsy's back and escorts him out of the room. Derkumon glances at Maladine just before closing the door. "Take care of her Maladine. Stay with her throughout the night. If she wakes again, fetch me quickly. I do not want her leaving in the night."

CHAPTER TWENTY-TWO

ERAMANE'S SEARCH

IT IS MORNING. THE SUN is beaming through an aperture above the bed I lie in. The light wakes me from my dreams of home, and the tightness and soreness of my body welcomes me back to my life now. Other than the stiffness in my muscles, in my core, my body has healed almost completely. Why will my mind not do the same? What I went through was horrible, yet I survived. How, though? Those wounds should have killed me. I have not harvested, yet still I live; now I must end him, the one that stole my life from me, the one whose presence resonates in my bones. I hear him in my thoughts. Something happened when I entered the Gate and bade it open; a path connected between Adikiah and me. Can he not hear me? It seems as though he does not; each emotion that comes through from him seems to stem from my loss into the Gate. Will he be with me always, raging and mourning in my thoughts? Is this the price I must pay for *becoming*?

I hear someone coming toward the door. It opens, and in comes the woman who helped me the night before. Maladine walks in and stops at my bedside. I sit up slowly; my stiff body objects. Humans hate and fear Adikiah, so why are they helping me? I do not know this woman, yet she tended me throughout the night. My body is hungry for a harvest. I look at the vulnerable housemaid. It would be an easy harvest, but as quickly as the thought enters, it leaves. My body heats at the shameful thought. Maladine puts her hand on my head. Her eyes widen and she jumps back in astonishment.

"You have a fever, child!" she exclaims, running out of the room, mumbling something about cold rags and onion paste.

I rise from the bed and put on the garment that Maladine left next to me. It is a solid black, leather piece that fits me like my own skin. It looks like something a thief would wear, not having anything loose on it, so as not to be caught by even a stitch. I look around and find a pair of boots beside the bed. Maladine, I guess, has braided my hair back. It must have been tangled, because it has been sheared several inches.

I leave the room and walk cautiously down a long passageway. There are no openings, only torches along the walls for illumination. I imagine the darkness of it at night, when the torches are extinguished. It would look much like the palace halls, dark and cold.

At the end of the corridor, I see the door to the galley, where cooks are buzzing around like a bunch of pollen-seeking bees fast at work to make their sweet honey. I walk pass the galley and head toward another door; apparently it leads outside. I see sunlight coming through a large crack at the bottom of the door, and as I reach for the knob, a hand grabs my shoulder. I turn and meet the gaze of the man touching me, fighting the urge to take his life. It is not a difficult fight; the man's stare calms me, lulls the rage that consumes me. I close my eyes and take a deep breath. Images of my two victims race through my thoughts—I grimace.

"Are you all right?" Limearsy asks. I am up against the wall and breathing so fast I feel like I am going to run out of air. I can feel their pain. It is just as torturous as the pain I felt when I passed through the Gate. "Are you all right?" he asks again. I come back to myself and look up at him. I regain my composure.

"Yes, I just need some fresh air." I say, flinging open the doors that lead outside.

I pause and let the sun shine down on my face. It is welcoming, as if to say, come outside, breathe the air, *live*! I have done such horrible things, and I believe I do not deserve to live at all. I feel guilt rise as I stand there letting the sun warm my body, my thoughts. I do not deserve to feel any pleasure or joy, because my victims can no longer feel pleasure or joy.

Although the sun is shining, the air is cool. Winter approaches and I am not looking forward to the cold. Past the bright shining sun, when my vision adjusts, I see a small gathering of rugged men, about twenty or so. They look like they are preparing for a battle. No wonder the bees in the galley are so busy. There are three of these men to my left, sharpening swords with a flat stone. One of them looks up at me.

"Is that her?" he asks Limearsy with a disappointed look on his face. "She looks about as tough as a three-legged dog," the man laughs as he spits at my feet. "She's no powerful thing at all," he continues on. "She does not look like she could hurt a dying beggar," he finishes with a sarcastic grin, turning to rally the other men. The crowd of brutes begins to laugh.

"Mind your tongue, Monte; she could kill all of you if she wanted. Now finish up; we need to move out soon," Limearsy commands.

"What is going on?" I ask.

"We have been waiting for you. We need you to help us find him," he says.

"Find who?"

"The Nameless One, the one who took you, the one who takes from us," he replies.

"Adikiah?" I interrupt. "These men, they know who I am? All of them?"

"Yes," Limearsy replies. I begin walking swiftly toward a horse. Limearsy grabs my shoulder. "Where are you going?" he asks.

"I'm leaving."

"You cannot leave," he exclaims. Limearsy grabs my arm with force, trying to stop me from mounting the nearby horse. Although Limearsy is a man, stronger than I remember any other man being, I am not intimidated. I just survived Adikiah, the Gate, and a fall from the heavens.

"Let me go," I demand. He does not comply. "Let me go, or I will kill you." My voice is calm and steady. He releases me. I stand there a moment, glaring into the eyes of the man, who for some reason makes me uneasy, makes me feel like maybe

I would not be able to kill him, and then I head for the horse again.

"You said yourself that you wanted him dead! Why are you trying to save him now?" Limearsy shouts at my back, following close behind. His question annoys me.

"I am not trying to save him! I am going to destroy him! Alone!" I shout as I reach for the saddle on the horse. Even though I do not truly feel I can overcome Adikiah, my desire for revenge, or retribution, or whatever emotion is compelling me to right what has been wronged, is unstoppable.

"Why do you not want our help?"

"Your *help*? You cannot help me. Those men know who I am, what I am; I cannot trust them, because they do not trust me. At any moment any one of them might try to attack me. Then what? Then I have to kill them ... I have to kill your men! They cannot help me. Adikiah will kill all of you!" His confidence makes me laugh aloud. "Your warriors cannot stop him," I say as I climb onto the tall black horse. "Even I may not be able to stop him," I finish. Limearsy grabs my stallion's bridle.

"No. We cannot leave without these men," he insists.

"Your men will die! They will all fall, and it will be because of you! You can save them by leaving them behind." He looks at me for a moment, then looks back at his warriors in waiting. "We will need some supplies for the horses." Limearsy grabs his horse.

"How far to the next town?" I ask.

"If we leave now, we will be there by dusk," he replies.

"Then we will get them there. If we do not hurry, these men will be ready and wanting to follow," I say as I settle into the saddle. Limearsy climbs on his horse behind me, and we ride off.

We demand much of the horses. They are starting to foam at the mouth, so we stop at the edge of the creek we are following. I sit under a giant moss tree near the bank while Limearsy leads the horses to the creek's edge. I tilt my head back, resting it on the willow. My thoughts are of Adikiah. I can feel his agony of being alone; he hates being alone, and after experiencing our time together, the loneliness overwhelms him. Until me, he had been alone for hundreds of years. I can hear his screams of regret, and I know that he feels sorrow for what he has done to me. His madness is enough to send any man to his knees, but because of his madness he cannot sense that I am still alive. I will never give him my pity; I crave revenge— for everything. Soon, though, he will settle, and then I will not have to seek him out; he will find me.

"We should reach the town of Grullom a short time before dusk," Limearsy breaks in. "We are making good time."

CHAPTER TWENTY-THREE

GRULLOM

A BREEZE GENTLY CARESSES MY skin, lightly blowing the hair on my body. It is soft and inviting, as if to say, "Come and dance with me." The sun is going down, and the evening has gone from an orange sunset to a thick gray veil covering the sky. The night is going to be long, but Grullom is just ahead.

The dim yellow glow of the street lanterns flickers as winds bluster through the streets. Not one person is out in the small, hidden town of Grullom. Limearsy does not seem to notice the absence of the townspeople; he just stares straight ahead.

After a moment, though, he breaks his silence. He has to shout, because the gusts of wind make a low whine as they pass. "My friend Hempshi lives just ahead! Follow me!" He rides ahead of me and gives his horse a squeeze to make it pick up its stride. My horse hurries to catch up without having been commanded. I follow him uphill until we reach a small, ivy-covered house. We dismount and walk the horses over to a watering trough. My giant black horse snorts as if to say, "Thanks for getting off my back."

After tying the horses, we walk on a narrow path of stones that leads to the door of this stone hut, secluded from the town. The door opens before Limearsy can knock, and a man inside grabs Limearsy, squeezing him tight.

"What brings you here, my good friend?" He steps back to get a better look at Limearsy, then leads us inside. "It has been so long; where have you been?" he questions Limearsy, shutting the door and looking at me for the first time. His eyes widen. "Where on earth did you find this glorious creature?" he asks with mischief and curiosity in his voice. The question from the short, fat, greasy pig of a man disgusts me.

"I am the furthest thing from glorious. If glory is what you seek, then you should turn to that big round belly of yours," I say without hesitation and feel immediate regret at my lack of regard. My insult puzzles Hempshi, so he shrugs me off and turns to Limearsy.

"Take anything you need," Hempshi says as he points to food sitting around the room. Hempshi is sure to be the town's baker, because his house smells of hot bread and fruit pies. "There is plenty of freshly cooked honey bread sitting on the warming stone over there." Hempshi points to a corner where a pile of flat warming stones heats the bread loaves. This man just offered Limearsy to take anything. I never offered Adikiah, and he took everything anyway.

"I did not come for your delicious breads, my friend; I came for horse feed," Limearsy says.

"You should take some food for you and your lady friend, Limearsy. You cannot exist on adventure alone," Hempshi says as he places some bread in a satchel and tosses it to Limearsy.

Hempshi leaves the room and returns after a few short moments. He hands Limearsy several small sacks of horse feed to give our hungry steeds. What I am hungry for I cannot have, but I refuse to harvest. For now, I have to control myself and live off of my sorrow and maybe some honey bread; it does smell delicious, and to my surprise the smell has caused my palate to water. I take all of the bags and walk toward the door; looking back at the man, I nod in gratitude. Hempshi's generosity is worthy of a mute thank-you.

The guilt I carry is a constant strangling sensation, a reminder of my profoundly harmed soul trying to reach out. I do not need a reminder. My soul wants to rest; I want to rest. I secure the feed while Limearsy is on the front stoop saying good-bye to Hempshi. After a quick couple of words, Limearsy starts for his horse. He is carrying several sheathed swords on his back; unless he had an arm for each of them, they would do him no good, and even that would only slightly increase his odds. Again, I find amusement in his confidence. We mount our horses and continue on our path to the Dark Forest.

We stop at the edge of the forest. Tall trees stand like guardians, protecting outsiders from the darkness they harbor. Humans fear it because of its legend, fairy tales rumoring the forest to be alive, an evil presence commanding it. To humans

these tales are only make-believe, but the idea of the tales is
what terrifies them. I look up at the mammoth trees and hope
that this place has no special powers; there will be only one
way to know for sure. "It will take us two days to go around,"
Limearsy says. I look at the trees a moment longer.

"We do not have the time; we have to pass through," I say.
"I have been through worse and deserve whatever awaits me in
there." I look at the wooded gate and nudge my hesitant horse
to proceed.

CHAPTER TWENTY-FOUR

THE DARK FOREST: PART ONE

THE NIGHT IS DARKER THAN what one's eyes view in death, and the amiable smell of the homely town of Grullom has diminished. Limearsy does not talk much, so I have only my thoughts to pass the time, thoughts of my time with Adikiah, thoughts of the dreadful things I have done. My guilt grows stronger, and my stomach begins to churn so badly I think I might vomit; and I do. I vomit right in the middle of my private banter. Putrid vomit splatters across the forest floor. The sounds of my regurgitation reach Limearsy's ears. He turns his horse and walks it a few paces back to me. "Are you all right?" he asks.

"I am fine," I say feebly, trying not to choke. I catch my breath and wipe the bile off my face with my sleeve. I am sure that this is regret's way of making my soul suffer more. Do I even have a soul? I am unsure; I do not know what I am anymore. Before Adikiah changed me, I was an innocent human being. After he took me away from my home, I became a murdering monster. I could live a thousand years and never atone for my ill doings.

We continue and the steaming pile of vomit is most likely being investigated by a curious scavenger. Limearsy and I are riding alongside each other; our stallions seemingly take control of navigation. I can sense that Limearsy is concerned about me, or possibly he is only disappointed. I was created from a powerful being, yet I seem nothing more than a desperate girl trying to keep from vomiting.

I distract myself with thoughts of Limearsy. He has a gentle enough demeanor; he seems a quiet man who stays to himself. So why do I feel like there is more to him than this heroic manner he portrays? Then again, do my suspicions even signify anything when I am suspicious of myself? I constantly negotiate the "why" to my existence. Why did I not die when I *became*? Adikiah said that I have a gift; my father spoke of it as well. Why do I have a gift? I have so many questions about myself that I cannot answer, and here I am, asking more questions that I cannot answer about a person that I hardly know.

Limearsy's short hair is now wet from the rain that started moments ago. His vivid blue eyes haunt me each time I have to address them. They remind me so much of Lebis, and it pains me to look at him. Last night when he rolled me over in the mud, I thought for a moment that he *was* Lebis. He is responsible for my will to survive. I had to live just to find out if Lebis was alive. Of course he was not, yet the resemblance of their eyes is remarkable.

"The rain will only become more intrusive," Limearsy says as he reaches into a leather duffle. "Take this." He hands me a black, hooded cloak. I put the swathe around my body, feeling gratitude for its warmth.

"Is this the only one you have?" I ask.

"Yes … but please wear it. I am used to these downpours," he insists generously. His generosity summons my guilt. I feel I do not deserve his compassion. Shortly after getting the cloak situated around me, Limearsy stops his horse, and my horse again mimics Limearsy's steed without command.

"You have not yet offered your name," he says.

"Oh, you do not know it?" I ask in disbelief.

"I know it … it is just that you have not told me. I know who you are and what happened to you, but I thought it would be nice for us to have a proper introduction, that way we are not strangers anymore," he finishes with a smile.

"My name is Eramane," I say without pride and order my horse to move forward.

Limearsy remains silent as we travel, and my past easily moves to the front of my thoughts. I recall when Samiah and I were practicing sword fighting one hot summer day. We went to the pond where mother could not see from the house; she would have disapproved. "Ladies do not use swords, Eramane," she would say. Samiah struck a hard blow, and my sword bounced off of his, striking me against my leg. I received a significant cut. We were afraid to tell our parents, but Samiah knew that my wound needed proper care, so we went to the caretakers' and had one of the children bring us a few things to bandage it. I remember the burn of the disinfectant, the blood that ran down to my ankle, and the look on my brother's face, much like it was when I cut my foot on the broken vase. Mother never discovered my wound, likely because it was almost healed in two days, a detail that amazed both Samiah and myself.

My emotions overwhelm me as I reminisce, and tears begin to spill down my cheeks. I stop my steed, and amidst the pouring rain we sit. Numb and uncertain of anything, I let the salty tears stream down my face. Limearsy patiently waits for me to speak. Looking up at him with my blurred stare, I ask, "What am I?" He says nothing, a look of puzzlement on his face. "What am I?" I scream, as I sob in the pouring rain.

Limearsy needs to pull me from the abyss of madness that aims to swallow me. He walks his horse over to me, dismounts into the thick mud, and reaches up for me. I fall into his hands, and he helps me down from my stallion. There we stand, our feet sinking down in the wet earth. Limearsy stands me straight up and lifts my chin so that we are looking in each other's eyes.

"The forest is taking you, Eramane," he says, and a look of pity and concern lines his face. The rain rushes down his head, and he continues, "Your soul has been devastated." His voice grows stronger and seems to intimidate even the rain. "You are a young girl who was taken from everything she was and made to be everything she is not! You are the prey of a powerful creature!" His words may be true, yet my dark abyss engulfs me still. Limearsy continues to speak. "Eramane, you did not do those terrible things. Adikiah's creation did, not you!" It is comforting for me to know that I am not despised by everyone. Limearsy believes in me, and the words he speaks next tame my thoughts: "You did not ask for this, Eramane. He forced you to *become*.

He could never have swayed you; your will is too strong, your soul too pure," he says. How does Limearsy know of the becoming ritual? "He would have never been able to make you forget your true self, the real Eramane." His words sweep away my pitiful feelings to a more comfortable distance. I turn from him without saying a word and mount my horse. I pause for a moment, then give my horse a nudge to get him walking. Limearsy is not far behind.

The rain diminishes from a downpour to a bothersome drizzle. We have been in the Dark Forest for much of the night. "The moon is directly above us. We have traveled through most of it," Limearsy announces. It is the first either of us has spoken since the heavy rain. A thick fog has crept in, slowly surrounding us. It wraps around the trees like a snake on its prey. Webs of dead moss hang from the tree limbs, as if they are stretching down to reach for us. A low moan slithers throughout the forest. Limearsy does not seem to hear it. It could be that he does hear it but does not want to acknowledge it. Maybe he is not as unsoiled as I thought. Is it not possible that this ominous place is coming to have its way with Limearsy? Most likely this is just an entertaining thought for me—a distraction from what I feel approaching.

The groaning takes back my attention. I listen, looking around to locate the source of the unsettling groan. Limearsy looks at me for a moment and then searches our environment, returning his focus to me, a look of concern on his face.

"What is it?" he asks. I do not answer immediately. Instead I continue to listen a moment longer, hearing nothing.

"Nothing," I finally reply. Silence takes over, and the fog grows thicker. Moments pass and then the groan begins again. This time the noise sounds as though it, not Limearsy, were the one riding beside me. We can hardly see each other because of the dense fog.

"Eramane, bring your steed closer," Limearsy requests.

"You hear it, then?" I ask for confirmation. The sound does not silence because of our exchange of words. Our horses become frightened and begin prancing around, disobeying our commands. Louder and louder the noise intrudes. At the moment that it seems as though the noise cannot get any louder, the ground begins to shake, and the winds blow fiercely.

We give our horses a more forceful command, to run as fast as they can, but the forest is too dense for a full-out gallop. I cannot see Limearsy's face, but I know what he is thinking, the same thing I am thinking, that something terrible is here, and it has come here for me.

Our horses slow in pace, then stop altogether. The stallions rear up, trying to dump us. The noise is so loud that it is not a groan anymore but a loud humming vibration that I can feel in my bones. It is as if the forest is screaming at us—all the trees, all the plants, every living thing, orchestrating this unbearable noise.

I feel something strike at me on my right side. It is the wind, trying to throw me from my steed. It must be the wind; nothing else is here. Just then, another strike; this time it has a face. I do not see it well, because it moves too swiftly. Then again it comes; this time I see it clearly. It is the distorted face of a boy. He strikes me so hard that I fall from my horse onto the ground with a shocking thud. The boy lunges on top of me, perching on my chest. His knees stretch up past his head. *What a wicked face,* I think, trying to figure out what this *thing* is. The evil monstrosity grabs my throat. His face is a pale blue color, and his eyes are blood red. He begins chanting words—words I do not understand.

A demonic voice blasts from the being, like the screeching of a colossal owl. His face begins to melt as he shrieks, as if it were on fire. His words jumble together, no breath taken between any of them, and he begins gashing my face and neck with his talonlike claws. It is all happening so quickly. Limearsy jumps off his horse and darts for me, but the forest has a different plan for him. Branches from nearby trees bend and stretch their way to Limearsy, grabbing him and wrapping him up in their wooden arms.

I throw the being from atop me and roll over to catch my breath. A breath is not what I get. Instead, the boy forcefully rolls me over. I look up at the foul being and watch as he drives Limearsy's sword through my abdomen and into the ground. I scream louder than all the mayhem that the devil child brought with him. Then it grows quiet.

I lie on the ground gasping and spitting blood. It gurgles in the back of my throat. I turn my head to Limearsy, my vision blurred by the blood from the gashes on my head; it makes it difficult to see him. "Eramane," he calls. "Eramane, I'm coming, hold on." He cuts away at parts of the tree that still constrict him. "Hold on," his words fade off, carried by the breeze. Then there is darkness.

CHAPTER TWENTY-FIVE

THE DARK FOREST: PART TWO

"ERAMANE," A VOICE CALLS TO me. I open my eyes to see Limearsy. Raising my head, I see the sword that pins me to the ground. My head drops back to the ground, and I sigh in annoyance. "Why did you not pull this from me while I was unconscious?" I ask, irritated.

"You woke before I reached you," Limearsy says.

"Well," I exhale laboredly, "get a firm stance and grab the handle .On three we pull." Limearsy does as I ask with little hesitation. "Ready? One, two, three!" He pulls and I scream in agony as the sword releases me. I roll on my stomach and scream into the dirt. I smash the ground with my fist, as if punishing the earth for my pain. Limearsy watches, unable to help, until I no longer writhe about. After a few moments, he helps me sit up.

"I know your wounds heal quickly, but not quickly enough, considering where we are," he says. "Ride with me;

we can hitch your horse to mine." I do not argue, as Limearsy is already preparing me to climb up on his stallion. "Sit tight, I am going to fetch your horse," he says, walking to my steed. Limearsy is swift and with no time wasted he is situating himself behind me. I hold onto his shoulders as we make our way through the Dark Forest.

We have been riding only a short time since my attack. I keep thinking about my family, holding onto to hope that they are still alive. I want badly to see them, to tell them how sorry I am. When I saw my father in the Gate, he said that Samiah and my mother need me. But I do not know what that means or even if I really spoke with my father at all. The look in Samiah's eyes when he fathomed my new existence tears away at me. I know that he cannot believe what I have become, and I cannot be convinced that the look on his face would have been any different had I pulled his heart from his chest. For the first time in my life, I saw tears in his eyes. Underneath the overwhelming emotion, though, I knew that he was not angry with me. Instead, he was devastated; as if he believed it was his fault. I think about Limearsy's words, of me being forced into this life, but I can never be the Eramane I was before the meadow, before Adikiah. Although I have a newfound hope, I know that no kind of redemption will make me the person I used to be. I am broken now, damaged. But I want to be reunited with my family, and that is enough to keep me strong.

Once we make our way out of the Dark Forest, we stop for a short time to feed and water the horses. With the Dark

Forest behind us now, I would like to imagine never having to pass through it again.

Adikiah told me that I will never again be human, my soul is tarnished. My sins cannot be forgiven by my gods, and I can never again be at peace with the humans; they will hunt me until the end of time and never cease in their vengeance. These are the terrible misfortunes I have to shoulder. I am not living yet not dead, and although I made it through the Gate, my existence is uncertain. I do suppose that Adikiah is likely to end me, but this is not enough for me to back down. I am told that I possess a gift, and I plan on uncovering its mystery—somehow. Although I cannot move mountains, I can make them quake. Yet none of this will matter if I do not harvest again. Eventually my energy will diminish, and I will be no more of a threat than a bothersome gnat. I had taken an immense amount of damage by Adikiah, the souls in the Gate, and the soul in the Dark Forest. If I am going to take on all that lies ahead, I should need to harvest. But I have made it this far, and, oddly enough, I feel strong. It does not make sense that I am not feeble, but here I am, healing from the demonic child in the Dark Forest. Now that I think on it, it is very odd. I should have been dead several times over. Something has given me strength to heal, to fight, and to live—but what? My focus turns to Limearsy, still scanning our path ahead; like a stone guardian, he rides in silence. He rides without even a scratch. I watched those branches violently scratch at him, and he is not even bleeding. What is going on?

As I ponder Limearsy's unscathed body, I cannot help wondering where Adikiah is. Certainly he knows by now I am

alive. I feel him; can he still not feel me? Why is he not hunting me? I hear his screams of remorse; I know he mourns me
still, an obsession he cannot let go of so easily. Where are you,
Adikiah? Why have you not tried to reach me? What are you
up to? If he is not seeking me, then he already knows where
I am. I do not know if I should talk to Limearsy about this. I
still do not understand his motives for keeping me alive if we
succeed in destroying Adikiah. Will he not want me dead as
well? I am a threat also; I still need to "take from them," do I
not?

A short time ago, I decided I was able to ride my horse.
Since then, we have been riding hard through the night, but
suddenly I am bombarded by Adikiah's voice. It hits quickly
and is so profound that I cannot function. I have to slow my
steed because I know that I am about to fall from it, and I
do. Limearsy is in front of me and does not notice that I am
grounded until he hears me screaming. Adikiah's voice is so
loud that blood trickles from my ears. I squirm on the ground
like a worm bitten in half by a bird's sharp beak. I cry out in
agony, and as suddenly as it started, it ceases. Why does his
voice hurt me so badly? I try to calm myself so I can decipher what I heard from him. I stand and regain my balance.
The world has stopped spinning, and I am able to replay the
sounds in my head. I listen to them carefully, trying to cor-
rectly recollect them. As I slow it down, I realize that Adikiah
was not saying anything at all. Instead, it was the sound of
his emotional outburst, an ecstasy he experienced as he just
learned that I am alive. He has found me.

Limearsy helps me to my horse. "You sure do have a difficult time staying in your saddle," he says, forcing a half-hearted smile from me. He knows my internal struggle is great, and he feels no need to inquire about it. His only inquiry is whether I am all right. Once I acknowledge that I can ride, we proceed. What Limearsy does not know is that Adikiah has just discovered that I am alive.

CHAPTER TWENTY-SIX

Adikiah Sends the Servants

A SOMBER PRESENCE PERVADES THE palace. Adikiah mourns his mistake. He longs to have Eramane back, to
be together as they once were; even if it means an eternity of
pleading with her to come down from the landing. Much of
his time is spent in his nest atop the palace. He is there now,
searching for her, traveling the world with his mind. His attempts have not been futile, for he did reach her, discovering
that she rides toward the town of Lunlitch.

"It is time to show my love that she belongs to me,"
Adikiah says as he summons his willing servants. One by one,
they appear at Adikiah's will. Forming a circle parallel with
the stone columns that encase the terrace, the servants stand
quiet and attentive. The ocean breeze whisks the cloaks of the
creatures, exposing their scrawny figures, a deceptive feature of
these powerful creatures. They lack a muscular physique, but
their stature has no relevance to the strength of these beings.

Adikiah created them to serve him not only in his palace but also in his crusades, whatever they may be. This time, Adikiah will send them on a mission to destroy the peaceful town of Lunlitch.

"Eramane is nearing Lunlitch. She travels with a companion whom I do not wish to breathe the air of tomorrow. Kill everyone in the town, including her companion, and leave her there to relish the death of the innocents. Let me make it clear that if she is harmed, all of you will pay! Go! Now!" he orders, and the servants quickly leave the terrace. Adikiah lies down and awaits the news of his slaves. "If she will not come back on her own will, I will force her," Adikiah rants, having sensed my intentions of making our separation permanent.

The night does not have much time left to conceal the fate of Lunlitch. Unsuspecting of their demise, the innocent townsfolk sleep peacefully, in what is to be their last night. Families are tucked away cozily, with fires warming their bodies. Thick smoke puffs lift from the smokestacks atop the homes. A little boy dreams of the fishing trip he and his father had gone on, while a young girl dreams of her new dress. The night has intentions of peace; however, Adikiah's plans are not the same.

Creeping in like fog from the sea, the servants whip through each home like a plague. In truth, they are worse than a plague. Usually, not all suffer from fatal pestilence; nonetheless, everyone in Lunlitch will suffer. Nonchalantly the servants disperse, invading each dwelling as ordered. The evildoers do not discriminate in their murderous rampage. Adults and children lose their lives tragically and without regard. The carnage carries less remorse than swatting at a fly lingering around the fruit bowl. And with only slightly more intelligence than a fruit fly, his servants follow Adikiah's demands yet lose sight of their purpose. As they begin their massacre, they become overwhelmed in the gratification of their undertakings. Yes, they bring about a bloodbath; however, they leave Lunlitch without waiting for me. The entire reason for them to be there, and they leave without taking care of Adikiah's orders. Once they arrive back at the palace, they will be reminded of their forgetfulness in very painful ways.

Lunlitch is now silenced by death, and the aura of evil, along with dense fog, is all that remains in the town.

CHAPTER TWENTY-SEVEN

A DOTING REMEMBRANCE

AS NIGHT CONSUMES OUR TREK, my head is consumed by horrible memories. I see Lebis's body convulse under Adikiah's attack. The feeble man Adikiah offered me on the landing, and the young girl from the village, take turns alternating between images of my mother's eyes, wide with astonishment as she recognized me, the one holding a tight grip around her throat. I cannot let go of these devastating images. I find that I keep reminding myself that this is my burden and that I will carry it until I die. It is a mantra that helps me identify who I am, a reluctant realization.

You mean to destroy me, Adikiah breaks in. I check to see if Limearsy notices my disposition. He seems to be in his own world, just proceeding forward. *I am not going anywhere, my love; you know where to find me. Bring Limearsy; bring a thousand armies, Eramane. After I kill each and every one of them, you will have no one left but me.* His confidence does not surprise me. In the depths of his being, Adikiah believes that I will lose my battle of hatred for him, that I will bring all the forces of all the lands to defeat him and, in the end, give in to his will. But I cannot worry about that right now, for I must focus on keeping him out of my thoughts. How am I to do that?

A while later we are in the flatlands, and soon we will arrive in the town of Lunlitch. This is the town my father used to call the Eye. It is in the middle of our lands. I remember my father speaking of it when he would set out on his travels. He would usually meet with a travel companion at the Eye, because it was the middle point for them to meet. Once, when I was a small child, he brought a music box home for my mother. Even now I hear its melody. The delicate sound, the tune of its music brings me solace, and I let the song repeat in my mind as much as it likes, a much-needed distraction.

Limearsy breaks my thoughts and turns his horse back to meet at my side. As we ride on, Limearsy holds his tongue, as if there is no particular reason for him to drop lead and wait for me to ride up next to him. Our pace slows, and as we continue, I find myself looking at his face. He is handsome, and as I continue to stare at him, an odd feeling of familiarity comes over me. The longer I look, the more I cannot help but feel that I know him or have encountered him somewhere before. I stop my steed, and Limearsy halts his as well.

"What is wrong, Eramane?" he asks. I do not reply, as now we are both peering at the other intensely. "You question me. Why?" Limearsy continues. He knows of my doubt. Of course he does; I have been glaring at him with suspicion since we met.

"I question everything, Limearsy. You should as well."
I command my horse to walk forward. We will soon enter
Lunlitch.

I feel Adikiah's presence. Why would he not be here? He
knew that I was headed for this town. But there is also another
reason I feel that he is near—I smell blood. It is the unmistakable smell of human blood, blood of the innocent. The closer
our horses bring us to Lunlitch, the more I can sense the hor-
rific fate of the villagers. Will Adikiah be in Lunlitch waiting
to take me back and make me his once more?

"Do you smell that?" Limearsy asks. I inhale and notice
that I no longer smell the blood of humans; I can smell their
burning flesh. "There is smoke ahead," Limearsy announces.

"Yes, I can smell it. The village is on fire," I say, keeping
my steed in a steady direction on the path to Lunlitch. Horses
do not like the smell of smoke. As with most animals, it is
against their instinct to approach a fire. But today my horse is
not able to listen to his own instincts; he has to obey mine.

CHAPTER TWENTY-EIGHT

SMOLDER

THE GROUND RUMBLES LIKE THUNDER as horses dig their hooves into it. Mud is being slung everywhere as they trample the wet earth. The Riders are already filthy, and the journey has just begun. Samiah focuses on finding his sister, and his stern visage looks as though the coldest of winters froze him to the bone, and he can never be warmed again. Sadness stretches across his face. *My dear sister,* he mourns to himself, *if only I had not let you go with Lebis, our father would still be alive, and you would not be at the mercy of that beast.* Samiah's guilt and sorrow gnaw at him as he and his Riders make their way into the town of Lunlitch.

The mist that had once dusted the ankles of the horses emerges as a thick blanket, obscuring their view into town. Samiah scans the town and notices an absence of its people. Wondering if something is amiss, he leans over to Nahmas. "It does not feel right, the town is vacant."

"We have come here at a bad time. We cannot help these people," Nahmas replies. The four men know that something evil has come into the village. They know that the villagers are dead. Being Riders for as long as they have, they each know what it means when you ride into a village and no one is there to greet you. The silence is what really calls to the men. It is that quiet that only death brings, and this village has come face-to-face with it. Nahmas, Aurick, and Terrin ride close to Samiah always. He is their new lord, and in the current circumstances, the brothers feel it necessary to surround him. The Ghosts feel responsible for not protecting Lord Danius; they are not going to make the same mistake twice.

Samiah and his men walk slowly through the town. Aurick and Terrin enter a few homes and return to Samiah with the news of what they saw. Entire families have been massacred. "They look as if a wild animal got at them," Terrin explains.

"The children?" Samiah asks.

"They are all dead, my Lord. Even the animal companions were slain."

"These people had no chance," Samiah says, imagining the terror the villagers must have felt.

"One creature did not do this," Nahmas says, searching the town with his eyes as they continue on. Samiah's anger escalates, and all he can do is clench his jaws to keep from screaming out his rage. Aurick notices parts of a human lying near the road and alerts the other Riders. As they move through the dense fog, they discover more and more pieces of human remains. The parts of these innocent people lie strewn all over.

"We cannot leave this town in this state," Nahmas says to Samiah, expecting that his lord might want to carry on.

"No, we cannot," Samiah replies. "They are strewn every-where. Unwary travelers should not stumble upon this," he finishes.

"What are your orders?" Nahmas asks. Samiah looks around at the remains of the villagers. A lump forms in his throat. He imagines his hometown of Eludwid; it does not dif-fer from Lunlitch: quaint village, charming people. This could have easily been the fate of their home.

"Burn it. We will burn the whole damn thing down," Samiah orders as he commands his horse to take him to a nearby hut. Samiah reaches the small home and dismounts. "Search for any pitch, sulfur, petroleum, or spirits you can find. Anything that will easily ignite," Samiah shouts to his Riders as he enters the home.

He looks around the empty cottage and, at first, notices that the home looks only as though its owners left it for the day to venture out. This pleasant thought will not last. Samiah enters the rear of the home, where the family slept, and discov-ers that they too have become victims of the massacre. Samiah quickly locates a flagon of spirits and exits the home. He meets with the others, and they discuss how they will go about set-ting the entire town ablaze. They need to get the liquids spread out enough to consume the village.

"Aurick, take what you have and start soiling the main entrance to town. Terrin, take yours and pour it behind the homes near the tree line. Nahmas, douse these huts behind me; I will drench the bodies in the road. Since the village is small, housing about twenty families, the task of setting it ablaze should not be so difficult."

As Samiah orders, the men douse their areas. Samiah gives the town another look, as if to say good-bye, then strikes his sword against a stone to ignite the flammable trail he made.

Samiah and his men gather toward the end of the burning town and watch as flames engulf the village, home by home. The horses stand obediently as the brothers begin mumbling prayers for the deceased villagers. Samiah sits quietly, as if he is listening to the wind. Sometimes the wind will tell you things if you listen closely enough. Other times maybe the wind just blows, but now the wind is speaking, and it carries on it the arrival of his dear sister. It tells him that if he listens carefully, he will hear her. Therefore, Samiah listens, carefully and observantly, to the wind. He breathes the cool air through his flaring nostrils and fills his lungs with it. And, as promised, the wind delivers the sound of his sister; she is calling to him: *Samiah*. He looks ahead toward the end of town, through the haze of smoke, and sees someone sitting atop a horse, staring back at him. Samiah squints, trying to focus on the person's image. He commands his horse to walk forward a few paces; just enough to give his eyes the proximity they need to clarify the image. "Eramane!" he shouts.

CHAPTER TWENTY-NINE

MEETING AGAIN

SAMIAH LOOKS AT ME, QUESTIONING if it is really me or not. I cannot tell what he thinks; it looks as though he may be convincing himself that I am really here. But I *am* here, and I only want to embrace him and beg him to forgive me.

After we gaze at each other for a moment, I leave my horse, and Limearsy, and walk toward him. As I approach, I see that he believes his eyes. He jumps from his steed, landing face-to-face with me. He holds me in his sight for only a second before clutching me to his chest. I clutch back, relieved that he is alive, relieved that he does not hate me. Samiah begins to sob, an emotion shared by both of us. Tears rush from me in a release that I have been longing for, for what seems like an eternity. Finally, our tears slow, and I feel him searching my back, as if looking for something. I lift my head from his

shoulder and peer into his teary red eyes. "They are gone," I
say. He retracts his hands and looks at my face instead.

The thick smoke from the blazing village dances around
us like the veil on a boisterous bride. Samiah does not take his
eyes from me as I speak my words of remorse: "I cannot make
right the wrong that I have done. I cannot make you forgive
me, and I do not think you should."

"I do not blame you, Eramane," he says almost breath-
lessly. Samiah slumps a little. Silence gloats at our circum-
stance. My voice is choking back, and I cannot speak another
word until he says something else—anything.

"I wish to kill the one who took you from us," he says, and
I am relieved. I am ever so grateful to see him, to know that
Adikiah did not kill him.

"I am sorry, Samiah; I'm so sorry, brother." He grabs me
and pulls me in again, hugging me tight.

"I am sorry for not protecting you, my dear sister," he says
in emotion-choked tones. "I would give my life for you to
have yours again, Eramane," he sobs. "I would give it a thousand times for you," he says sincerely.

CHAPTER THIRTY

LIMEARSY'S REVELATION

THE MEMORY OF THAT DEVASTATED village trav-
els with us on the wind. We ride fast, all of us, but the carnage cradles us along the way. Samiah and the Ghosts look as
though a lifetime of blissful moments could not eradicate the
images of Lunlitch forever burned in their minds, poor souls.
I know I do not have much time before Adikiah imposes his
presence on my thoughts again. I do not know if I can keep
him out, but so far, I have kept him at bay.

Samiah's men are loyal and fight for him without question.
None of them challenged me as Limearsy and I joined their
clutch. Nahmas even gave me a caring smile when our eyes
met. I suppose I was not truly concerned with how the Ghosts
would respond to me; they have been part of my brother's life
long enough to call them family. I even walked with Nahmas
down the aisle at my brother's wedding. Although they have
not spoken to us, they give us no looks of distrust, and their

silence means little; they do not speak often. Still, I am thankful they have accepted my companion. Limearsy saved my life; I owe him my allegiance.

The brothers ride alongside of Samiah, remaining loyal to their oath as his protectors. I wonder how truly committed they are, if they will stand strong with him upon seeing Adikiah and his legion of sycophants.

Black skies and no sight of the stars are what I look at as I lie in hopes of rest. I need a rest that comes only in death. I yearn for it, almost as badly as I yearn to destroy Adikiah. But my mind will not settle on anything except the faces of my victims; I need something to take my mind off this burden.

"Limearsy, wake up," I whisper, trying to rouse my companion. He sits up instantly.

"I am not sleeping, Eramane. I cannot sleep, and I see that you are having troubles sleeping as well," he says, flames from the campfire dancing in his eyes. Those eyes, they are a blessing and a curse. While they remind me of Lebis's bright face, they also remind me of his death; the two do not exist as separate memories. I feel like his eyes are a connection to my past, but something else connects us. I sense it, and the longer I am in his presence, the more I am drawn to him, like leaves to the sunlight. Something within me constantly reaches for him.

He sits calmly. "What is it, Eramane?" he asks. The camp is quiet, but Limearsy and I both know that our words are not being ignored. Samiah and his men are undoubtedly holding their breath to make sure they do not miss a word. I lower my voice as much as possible so that we can continue our conversation.

"Nothing—and everything. It is just that I feel you are keeping something from me. I do not know what it is, but I know there is something. What is it?" I ask.

The wind sweeps through the camp before settling again. Limearsy shifts. What is the burden he carries? He leans closer, "By midday tomorrow, we will be in the Gwariff Forest." he says, as he rummages through his pocket. He pulls out a vial of liquid, resembling the one I was given when he found me. "You will need to drink this, Eramane, to keep up your strength. You have not harvested in days."

I look at him, just short of being angry. "I do not need to harvest, Limearsy. Look at what I have been through, and I have healed on my own. I do not need to take human life."

"I know, Eramane. I know that you do not wish to harvest," he says."

"I do not wish it. I will not harvest," I say.

"Eramane." He softens, putting the vial in my hand. "Just drink this, please," he urges.

"Limearsy, I do not need your elixirs." I push the vial back at him.

"You do, Eramane."

"No, I do not. Now take it or I will throw it!" I say. I have had my fill of vials and tinctures and concoctions. He moves in closer, much closer; our faces almost touch.

"Yes, you do. How the hell do you think you have made it this far without harvesting?"

"What are you talking about, Limearsy?"

"You have gained your strength from this, Eramane," he says putting the vial in my face. "I made it especially for you, so that you could live without having to take lives. Do you see?" he asks eagerly. I snatch the vial and hold it against the light of the small campfire. It is beautiful, tempting. I continue to examine the liquid, admiring it, desiring it. I find that my urge to consume the elixir is not much different than my urge to harvest.

"So, I am still like him," I say, tears welling. I remove the cork and consume Limearsy's elixir.

"You are not like him, Eramane," he says. I hand the empty glass vial back, putting it in his hand with a defeated sigh. Limearsy takes the vial and then grasps my hand; he squeezes it gently. "You are no more like that fiend than I am. Do not lose yourself again, Eramane. Just give the elixir some time; you will feel stronger soon. Trust me when I say this, Eramane." He clasps his hands around mine. "It is better for you than a harvest."

"Trust you? For all I know, you are just using me to defeat Adikiah, and then once I am weak, you will come for me too. And you want me to trust you? I do not even know you!" He looks at me, seeing straight through to my defeat.

"You can trust me, Eramane. There is no one else in this world that you can trust more than me, not even your brother; humans will always fear us." My eyes widen.

"What? Limearsy, what are you saying to me right now?" He does not hesitate to elaborate.

"My father is the one we seek to destroy. It is not only what you want, but I as well." He checks the others to see if there is any movement.

"Your father!" Sorrow engulfs me, and tears line my eyes. "I do not believe this." My words are sad and soft. It truly, deeply hurts. I knew he was keeping something from me, but in a thousand years I would not have suspected Limearsy to be the son of Adikiah. I do not want him to say any more, but my curiosity will not allow me to walk away.

"How?" I ask in amazement. "Adikiah never spoke of a child."

"My mother was human. One night my father came into her house, killed her husband, and planted his seed within her. From what I was told, he let my mother know that he was coming back for me, and if she tried to flee, he would kill both of us. Derkumon came to save me from my father and helped a group of men escape with me. He was badly wounded and left to die. That is how he lost his eye. He helped raise me and encouraged me to use my strength to destroy my father." Limearsy stands, "I am not like him, Eramane. I have a soul. I feel pain, love, hate, sadness, and loss, all of it. I even feel you. That is how I knew where to find you that night you lay dying in the mud," he says as he pulls me to him. "I received only strength from my father, nothing else. That atrocity has to die so that we can have peace."

"You do not have to harvest?" I ask resentfully.

"No, Eramane, but you do for now, which is why I have made these vials for you. They will help keep you strong while you learn how to summon your gift."

"My gift? What is this gift that I have? Adikiah spoke of it, and my father, and now you. What is it? I can shake things up a little, is that it? Because summoning tremors will not keep me alive!"

"It is so much more than that, Eramane." We have moved in so close that I can feel his breath on my face. "You are a Breather." I look at him, saying nothing. "Do you know what that is?"

"No."

"Well, to begin, there has not been a Breather in more than five hundred years." I listen intently. "A Breather can control anything in existence, once they have mastered their craft: humans, animals, vegetation, the elements of our world … you see?"

"You are saying that I can control anything I choose. You expect me to believe this? Because I surely do not feel like I can do anything close to any of that."

"You can believe it or not, but sooner or later, Eramane, my blood will deplete, those vials will run out, and you will have to harvest. If you do not learn how to seek your strength from your gift, you will be faced with a terrible decision."

"Oh, Limearsy," I say. "This is bad. I cannot take from you; I cannot survive that way. You cannot survive that way. I saw what it did to Adikiah when he gave part of himself to me."

"You have to, Eramane. If you do not harvest, you must take from me."

"And what does it do to you?" I ask.

"I will be fine, Eramane, as long as you are alive."

CHAPTER THIRTY-ONE

GWARIFF FOREST

GWARIFF FOREST IS A MOST enchanting place. It reminds me of the quaint place Lebis and I had our picnic. I have never been here before, and neither have the others that accompany me. Sunbeams come down from the sky and give a warm glow to the woods. Tree creatures scurry about their business to gather the last morsels before the frigid winter comes. The trees are barren, and the ground is blanketed with the leaves that once clothed them. If I were the Eramane I used to be, I would have been taken by the magic of Gwariff Forest. Now I look at it as a sad remembrance of Lebis.

Samiah and Nahmas lead us on the narrow trail we follow through the forest, and the other two brothers trail us. Limearsy and I ride side by side, as if we are two children on our way to be punished for ignoring our chores and running off to frolic in the woods, not to be heard from all day. We have not revealed Limearsy's secret to Samiah or the others; I am sure they would not be accepting of his true identity. They do not know that he truthfully despises their Nameless One as much as they do, and I certainly have not mentioned that I supposedly possess a gift that has been absent from the world for centuries. If they find out that Limearsy is the natural child of Adikiah, they will attack him, and I will lose my brother or be forced to fight Limearsy. I am not sure what strengths Limearsy possesses, but if he is anything like his father, he is enormously powerful, which leads me to wonder. "How have you managed to keep disconnected from your father all of these years?" I ask.

"Well, at first Derkumon sought help of an impression caster. They helped shield my existence from him until I was old enough to control it myself."

"I see."

"Eventually I learned that I could hear him, sense him when I wanted, without him detecting me. That is how I discovered you, Eramane." Limearsy tells me of his mother and how her purity was passed on to him. "Derkumon said that this was the reason they knew they could raise me as one of their own." Limearsy continued to tell me that Derkumon taught him how to focus his thoughts by listening to the sound of his breath. "I would get so worked up trying to control the barrier between me and my father that I would feel like my mind was going to explode."

"Do you think you could teach me?"

"Surely," he says, smiling. This cheers me a little, and I decide to ride up next to Samiah.

I gallop my horse to Samiah and slow it to meet his pace. He looks around the wooded area intently, then realizes I have joined him. "I was wondering when you were going to join me," he says. He looks at me briefly, then back to the forest. "Did you witness what became of Lebis?"

I hang my head before answering, "Yes, I did." I can see that my dear brother feels pity for me.

"Did that ... *thing* ... hurt you?" he asks, as he tries to swallow the lump in his throat.

"Yes ... more than I could describe to you, more than you could bear to hear." Samiah is silent for a moment, then speaks again.

"What is it?" he asks exhaustedly. I take a short time to find the words.

"His name is Adikiah. His kind has been around since the beginning of it all. His true form is the creature you saw. It is what he becomes in order to harvest, the form he was when he killed Lebis and took me."

"I cannot imagine how frightened you were," Samiah says sympathetically.

The sound of dried leaves and twigs snapping under the horses' feet fills in our silence. Every once in a while a horse will snort, but that is the only noise. After a few silent moments, I continue to elaborate on the beast they call the Nameless One. I think it will be best if Samiah does not know details of my stay with the hideous fiend he has been forced to hate so deeply; therefore, I do not tell him of them.

"He is very powerful, Samiah, and truly there is no reason for you or your men to be here right now. You are no match for Adikiah," I say.

"Have you told your companion this, Eramane?" Samiah asks quickly.

"Limearsy is with me for reasons I cannot say," I reply. "But yes, I urged him to rethink his decision to accompany me."

"Shall he fall easily as well?" Samiah asks. "If you think that I could let this go and wait for my sister and someone I do not know to avenge my family, then you are mistaken, Eramane. I would rather die to avenge our father and Lord Danius than do nothing," he firmly states.

"Mother?" I utter, sadly remembering what I did to her. I have assumed that she lives since Samiah has not spoken of her as though she is dead. My grief is overwhelming and tears fall down my face as I ride next to my brother in silence.

"She lives," Samiah offers relief.

"How does she feel about her daughter?" I ask, wiping at the steady stream of tears.

"That beast is responsible for all of this, Eramane; I know this, and so does she. Mother loves you and misses you. She only wants you to return home, alive and safe."

Again our words cease for moments, and I begin to look at the surroundings. Even though Samiah assures me that our mother still has love for me, I still harbor immense grief for the pain I have caused her.

Once we pass through Gwariff Forest, our journey will not take us much farther. Adikiah lives near Gwariff Forest, and I am sure that he waits for us. He has no reason to fear us or send a legion to keep us away. He does not know Limearsy is his son, and that his son wants to end him.

We leave the protection of the forest and are making our way to the shore. It is dark now, and we will have to follow the shore for a little longer before reaching the palace. I am very curious to know what Limearsy holds within. The more I think of what powers he might possess, the more I realize that we really have a chance of defeating Adikiah. I take a deep breath and try to regain my *self.* I still have a part of that innocent girl in me. That is where my true strength resonates. As long as I keep hold of her, Adikiah will never succeed in making me his.

CHAPTER THIRTY-TWO

A PALACE NOT DIVINE

THE MOON IS NOT OUR friend tonight; it gives off no light. Not the way it illuminated the palace chamber, when it was so plump and bright. Tonight it seems as if the moon is in hiding, afraid of what will soon transpire. The six of us stand at the edge of the ocean, gazing at Adikiah's home. The giant mountain looks as if it is floating in the churning waters. The perfect location for protection: if one cannot fly, then one must risk the volatile sea. Ocean waves crash against the massive rock as if trying to penetrate the palace walls, a familiar sound. I close my eyes and remember the first time I listened to the raging water. It seems so long ago, and I pray that those moments are gone forever, that we will defeat Adikiah and that I will never be forced to relive them.

The mist that has followed me since the beginning of this journey of atonement has made its way out to sea and surrounds the fortress, as if it were the guardian of the palace. It pleases me to know that I am on my way to destroy Adikiah.

"We must swim it. There is no other way," Terrin says after a long silence. None of us want to hear it aloud. The waters are frigid and forbidding and will be unforgiving to our need for warmth, yet the desire for revenge is powerful; it will take more than a cold swim to deter us.

"Once we reach the palace, we will have to make our way up and into the nethermost regions. It will be dark, so stay close," I inform the men.

Halfway through our swim to the mountain, Aurick begins to fall prey to the freezing waters. "My hands and feet are numb. I cannot feel them," he says in exhaustion. He spits water out of his mouth as he speaks, and we all know that if we do not get him to the rocks at the bottom of the palace, he will perish in the sea. Limearsy is closest to Aurick and swims over to help. "Hold on, Aurick, I am coming."

By the time Limearsy reaches Aurick, he is almost completely numb and cannot swim on his own. Limearsy takes hold of Aurick and lugs him the rest of the way. Once we make it to the rocks, the climb to the entrance is not too far. The rocks are slippery and make it difficult to climb, and the higher up we get, the more likely fatal a fall will be. Aurick's trek is even harder, because he has lost feeling in his hands. He reaches for a rock hold that does not have enough room for him to grip. He shakes as he extends to grasp it; unsteady he swings over to it. His hand grabs the rock and then slips off.

"Ahh!" Aurick shouts, falling past me. Limearsy is below. He extends his arms and snatches Aurick just before it is too late. "By the gods, man, thank you," Aurick says, regaining his grip.

We make our way into the palace and reach the fire pits, where the fires blaze intensely and lavish our bodies with heat. Each of us takes advantage of their warmth while we dry out ripped pieces of our clothes in an effort to construct torches. "They will not last long, so let us make good use of them," I say.

"I can feel him," Limearsy says quietly.

"Then we both do," I reply.

"We all do," Samiah adds. "No one could be numb to this heavy air. That monstrosity's presence fills this place," he finishes. Samiah and his men begin to discuss a way to strategically search the domain for Adikiah.

I turn to them. "He knows we are here. He knows that we are using his fires to fashion torches. He waits for us in the Gate chamber, and that is where we must go to find him," I conclude.

"What is the Gate chamber?" Nahmas asks.

I look at Limearsy. "It is where I came from before Limearsy found me." I turn to the others. "Every soul that we harvest goes there. Good or evil, they are all there, and if you go near the Gate, they will pull you in with the force of a thousand horses."

We make our way down the corridor that will lead us to the chamber where I know Adikiah will be waiting. I have heard Adikiah since we plunged into the icy waters surrounding the palace. He told me where he would be waiting for us. It seems as though he is excited, thrilled with the matter at hand. He absolutely believes that he will kill my brother, the Ghosts, and Limearsy, and then he will have me again. I feel very strong in this place, and although I have not harvested, I trust Limearsy's promise that the elixir he gives me is better for me than a harvest. We will soon find out.

I lead Limearsy and the Riders down the narrow walkway, listening to the familiar sound of water trickling down the rock walls. When I am aware that we have reached our destination, I stop and turn to Limearsy and my brother. "This is it," I say. I try not to show my emotions to my brother; my tears will not make him turn from this place. I just cannot see a way for Samiah and his comrades to escape this battle with their lives. Samiah tries to enter the chamber. "No!" I plead and grab the handle. "Please go back, Samiah! Please take the Ghosts and leave before it is too late," I beg of him. His hesitation gives me false promise that he will heed my request, and then he responds.

"I am not leaving here without you," he says. He turns to the Ghosts. "Nahmas, Terrin, Aurick, you are my brothers…"

"If you fall here, we shall all fall here," asserts Nahmas. Terrin and Aurick affirm their brother's claim and pull their weapons. I rest my head on the big wooden door for a moment, and in that instant I gather all of the strength I can summon to carry on.

"Well, let us not keep him waiting," I say as I open the doors that will expose my companions to the force they must now reckon with.

CHAPTER THIRTY-THREE

SERAPH

WE STAND ACROSS FROM ADIKIAH; he remains seated. The room is larger than I remember. Adikiah's servants form a crescent behind his throne, all of them looking down at the floor. They seem to be new to the palace; they stand apprehensive, not knowing what to expect from their new master.

"Did you murder the others as you did in the relic chamber?" I ask, commenting on the sheepish bunch. Adikiah makes no expression.

"I recruited a new lot. The others disobeyed. They were supposed to retrieve you from that little town after they slaughtered everyone. Obviously, they did not bring you home, and they paid with their lives." Cinders smolder in a deep fire pit that separates us from our adversary. Our attention is immediately drawn away from Adikiah when the wall flanking us begins to pulsate.

"The wall is … breathing," Terrin announces.

"That is the Gate?" Samiah questions.

I nod my head. "That is it," I say.

"Well, my love, who are my guests?" Adikiah asks impishly. He steps down from his mighty throne, flexing his body, stretching himself out, preparing to turn into the creature that he is. He walks to the edge of the fire pit. "Hello, brother," Adikiah says laughingly from across the fiery crevice; he fixes a stare on Samiah. "Tell me, how is your father, and that lovely mother of yours?"

"I did not come here to exchange words. Cross that pit and fight!" Samiah demands. Adikiah's slow, deep laughter echoes through the chamber.

"Fight?" He continues laughing. "Why do we need this quarrel? Has not Eramane come back to my home, where she belongs?"

"No, beast, she has not come back to you," Samiah says. Adikiah paces in front of the pit that separates us from him. As he passes each of my companions, he glares at them, taking in their worth. He reaches Limearsy and halts.

"You are the one who found her? You nursed her wounds, comforted her when she was weak?" Adikiah's chest heaves with distaste.

"I am the one that saved her from the death you sent her to," Limearsy says unwavering.

"You saved her, did you? Tell me, then—why did you bring her back here to me?"

"I came back here to end you," I interject. Adikiah moves his focus from Limearsy and positions himself across from me.

I feel my body begin to tremble. He looks me over, and I watch his expression move from inquisitive to distraught.

"Where are your wings?" His forehead wrinkles with concern.

"They were torn from me in the Gate passage," I say coldly. He clashes his teeth together, and his nostrils flare.

"I am sorry for that; they were beautiful," he says woefully.

"Enough!" Samiah bellows. "Why are you hiding behind these flames? Will you stand there, or will you fight?"

"Your brother wishes to die tonight, Eramane. He is willing to die ... for what?" Adikiah pries.

"You killed our father! You took my sister and forced her to into a life meant only for foul things such as you! That is why I am here! Now cross this pit and fight me, damn you!" Samiah's rage is untamable and if Adikiah does not cross the pit soon, Samiah will risk jumping it.

"Yes, I took her. Yes, I killed your father, but I did not force her to harvest; she chose to live, so she chose to kill. You see, brother, she did choose this for herself," Adikiah gloats. He does not relish his pride for very long; Nahmas shoots an arrow into his abdomen. Adikiah looks surprised; it went in deep. He grasps the shaft and pulls the arrow from him, and his face contorts. "Shall we, then?" Adikiah remarks as he transforms from his beautiful human form into his wretched beastly self.

Just as I have witnessed many times, my comrades look on in awe as Adikiah's bones stretch and his skin blackens. Horns force their way from his skull, forming weighty armor on the sides of his head, and in seconds there he is, the beast they call the Nameless One. Adikiah's true form emerges and he spreads his wings like the massive sails of an ocean vessel. Adikiah, not wanting to offend Samiah any longer, jumps the wide pit with ease and lands with a hard thud in front of my brother. Without hesitation Adikiah grabs Samiah by his throat, lifting him from the ground. The Ghosts charge the fiend. Adikiah defends himself with his wings, hitting Terrin and Aurick with calculated strikes, sending them across the chamber and into sharp edges of the nearby wall. Nahmas shoots as many arrows as he can at Adikiah, but they do not pierce his flesh this time. "Your friend wishes to die," Adikiah says to Samiah as he tightens his grip on my brother's throat. The mighty beast reaches into the fire pit, breaking off a piece of hot wall rock, pulling it from the pit. He hurls it at Nahmas, who shields himself but is knocked off his feet.

"Eramane, come back to me and I will make this end!" Adikiah pleads. I look for Limearsy and see that he is out-numbered by the servants. They claw and lash out at him; one moves in and sinks its teeth into Limearsy's shoulder. Where are the Ghosts? It is difficult to see everyone because Adikiah has thrown several fiery rocks about the chamber, smoke ob-scures the area. If I do not attack quickly, my brother will suffocate under Adikiah's grip. I lunge at Adikiah, hoping that I will loosen his grip so that Samiah can break free of it. I hit him and make an escape possible; Samiah gasps for air and stumbles back. My hold is strong and Adikiah's only defense is to pull me into him, a move I did not anticipate. Now I am the one losing air beneath his forceful squeeze. If I do not escape his hold, I will lose consciousness. My eyes open and shut as I fight against him. In between their shuttering, I see that Limearsy has taken down the servants, all of them. *That is amazing* is all that crosses my mind just as I am about to slip away from reality.

I can breathe again! My eyes open and I get my bearings; I have fallen to the ground. I look up and see Adikiah fall back, using a wing to cover his face. The assault came from Aurick, hardly visible. He traced and became a sheer reflection of himself, as if he were made of water. With all the commotion, and the smoke, Adikiah was unable to detect his faint image. Aurick blew a powder on Adikiah's skin that engulfed his flesh, causing an unfathomable burning sensation. I hear him scream; not aloud, but I hear it.

Now we have Adikiah surrounded; Limearsy has rejoined after eliminating the servants. Each of the brothers has traced, and I can see that Adikiah wishes for better odds. His confidence has minimized with the defeat of his servants and Aurick's sneak attack.

"Is this how you envisioned my return, Adikiah?" I yell to him. He slowly pulls his wing away, revealing his face. Not a hint of damage can be seen.

"Is this how you envisioned my defeat, a few casters and two warriors?" His words turn to a laugh, but his banter is short-lived. He is no longer interested in toying with his prey.

Adikiah charges me, pushing off with a powerful thrust; there is nothing my comrades can do to stop him from reaching me. He snatches me up, like an owl swoops in on a field mouse, and just I was before, I am engulfed by his strong arms and massive wings. He wraps his wings over me, making a cocoon. He looks at the others and looks to the pit of fire. Each of my comrades must know his intentions; I can hear them as if I were the one thinking them; Adikiah is going to jump into the pit, where no one can go in after us.

He makes his estimations, where he stands, where my comrades stand. I try to free myself, but his might is greater, a fact I have always known yet stubbornly denied. *What a foolish underestimation, Eramane.* I fear what the flames will feel like, even though I know Adikiah will help me to heal; it will be an unimaginable pain nonetheless. I begin to cry, as I cannot hold back my fear; I am terrified. Adikiah darts for the pit, and I scream my objection. The familiar tingle surges through me, coming on faster than it has in the past. I feel Adikiah's body absorbing it, flinching against it. *I will get to that pit before you can rip us apart, Eramane.* I feel weightlessness as we leave the ground, plummeting into the fire. Just before I lose sight of my brother to the depths of the pit, I see him diving over the ledge after us, his sword pointing down, aiming for Adikiah.

CHAPTER THIRTY-FOUR

THE ORB

THE GHOSTS AND LIMEARSY STARE down into the pit in astonishment, the stench of defeat smothering them. "I could not seize him quick enough. I did not expect him to charge after them," Nahmas says, his voice dry. Limearsy cries out for Eramane, but the flames give no reply.

"That is it? Just like that the beast takes our brother, and we are left in shame?" Terrin says, unable to accept their loss.

"We cannot stay here. It is over, we must leave," Aurick says, pulling his brothers away from the edge. Terrin goes with him; Nahmas gestures to Aurick for a moment alone with Limearsy.

"Come, my new friend. We can do nothing for them now. Accept that they are at peace; that should give you comfort. Our friends died a death that will allow their souls to move from this world. We should be grateful they were not taken by the beast." Limearsy knows that he cannot save her, and he turns from the pit.

The men almost exit, but the Gate chamber brightens, and it catches Limearsy's attention. He turns and sees that a fire orb has ascended from the pit. It is large, the size of thousands of candle flames. The orb floats up until it comes to a rest on the chamber floor. The Ghosts have followed Limearsy back into the room, witnessing the phenomenon. After a moment, the orb's flames begin to suffocate, snuffed out by the force that drives it from its core. The flames vanish, and what remains is Eramane, standing strong and mighty. She holds her brother in her arms; he is lifeless and afflicted with burns on various parts of his body.

"Give me all of your vials, Limearsy," she says, laying Samiah gently on the ground. He is unconscious and the burns to his face would indicate that he is dead. "Please, hurry!" Eramane shouts. Limearsy hands her three vials of his tincture, although he is reluctant.

"They are the last," he says, knowing that it does not matter, that she would give her life for Samiah's. She empties each of the vials into his mouth and holds his head.

"Will they work?" Eramane asks.

"They should; he is human, though, so I cannot be sure," Limearsy admits. She rubs Samiah's head, trying to rouse him. She looks him over, searching for any sign that the concoctions are working, and then she sees it; the patches of burnt flesh on his cheek are beginning to repair themselves.

CHAPTER THIRTY-FIVE

RENEWAL

WE ALL STAND BACK TO give him room. In moments Samiah's skin has renewed itself; I can see no blemishes. He begins to cough and shake a little, but in a short amount of time, he is able to stand.

"So, that is what three will do," Limearsy says. Samiah looks at me for the second time in disbelief.

"How are you alive?" he asks. He puts a hand to his face. "How am I alive?"

"You saved her, and then she saved you," Nahmas says. Samiah reaches for me, and I walk the short distance to him. He pulls me in and clings to me, desperate to never let go. Our elation from Samiah's revival has us unaware of the beast that is clawing his way to the top of the pit, until he has me in his grip. This time, he squeezes me so tightly that I will soon lose consciousness. With Samiah too weak to fight, Limearsy and the Ghosts may again risk their lives for me. *You have proven yourself powerful to these mortals, but amidst all your glory and your greatness lies your weakness,* I speak to Adikiah through my thoughts.

What is that, my dear Eramane?

"Me," I declare, and my eyes open wide. Adikiah's eyes bulge and his mouth gapes as I draw my hand from his chest. Adikiah does not have a heart, but he does have a life source. I saw it the day I *became,* pulsing in the middle of his chest.

I hold the faintly glowing red orb in my hand as I step away from him. He stumbles back a few steps and uncontrollably shifts from one form to another. He shrieks so loudly that the palace begins to quake. I toss the organ into the bright orange coals and run toward my comrades; I do not make it. A large rock falls from the chamber ceiling and smashes on top of me, pinning my crushed body beneath it.

I lie lifeless and unable to move. I cannot scream. I cannot breathe. I cannot think. All I can see is the devastated look on Limearsy's face as he falls to his knees. "Eramane!" Limearsy yells.

My life is fading and my breathing is faint, but I am alive enough to watch in amazement as Limearsy changes into the form he inherited from his father. The speed of his transformation is similar to his father's, occurring in only a few seconds, but the resemblances cease there. Limearsy buckles as his bones enlarge. His skin loses its color, turning a pale gray, like dried stones that protrude above the water's surface on a hot day. He reaches the height of his father, and bulks to match his size. Limearsy does have wings and leathery skin; his flesh is like marble, an impermeable armor. His human characteristics remain, but his eyes shimmer like diamonds, colorless, gleaming, as they appear when hit with sunlight. It is an amazing sight; his form is intriguing, fearsome.

"*Beast*!" Limearsy cries. Adikiah has no chance of defeating him. "You will bleed for what you have done, Father!" Limearsy declares and charges Adikiah, who remains motionless, taken by Limearsy's revelation. He does not try to defend himself as his son attacks. Limearsy hits his father with great force, sending Adikiah into the wall behind him, the Gate.

Adikiah screams in anguish as hands pull him in and wrap around his flesh. Adikiah wails again and again. Every plea for mercy is fainter than the last, until they are not heard at all.

Limearsy rushes over to me and pushes against the boulder. The Ghosts and Samiah have been trying to push it from me, but they cannot budge it. Limearsy can move this rock, though; and at a single push it rolls enough to slide me from beneath it. Samiah falls beside me and cries out for mercy. How many times can one lose one's sister in a lifetime? The palace takes to quaking again, and pieces of rock begin falling. I am not to blame for the trembling walls this time.

"We must leave now," Nahmas says. Limearsy takes me into his arms and rushes with the rest of the Riders out of the palace. The mighty palace falls apart quickly as my companions make their way back to land, swimming back with a bit more ease, for the tide moves with them, pushing them to shore. Limearsy is easily able to carry my limp body to the shores; he has not shifted back to his human form.

Limearsy puts his hand on my chest and closes his eyes. He needs not speak to do what he is doing. Keeping his hand on my chest, he leans over and kisses life into me. I gasp and take in the salty air. Limearsy sits me up and the others stare at me in disbelief. I look around for a moment, not knowing where I am or what happened. Then I look up at the seraph leaning over me. "What happened? Limearsy, you ..." I lose my words.

"Yes, I brought you back," he says, rubbing sand from my face. Samiah crouches down to me; he lifts his hand to my head. I feel something rub against my scalp. He removes his hand and I take its place with mine. My fingers find a metal hairpin, my bird-wing hairpin. I sit up and wrap my arms around my brother. "Thank you," I say, "for saving me." I look back to Limearsy. "Is Adikiah ...?"

"He is in the Gate now," Limearsy says. "With eager souls waiting to greet him; they will tear at his flesh until nothing exists anymore." I take a deep breath, and for the first time since my picnic with Lebis, I feel free. I cannot hear Adikiah in my thoughts any longer, and I wonder how long it will take him to free himself from the Gate, as I did.

Eramane X Book Two

Prologue

THE MEADOW SMELLS OF THE fresh blooms opening across its spread. As far as I can see, the tiny lavender flowers speckle the field. A gentle breeze blows strands of hair over my eyes, blocking my vision for a moment. When the breeze lets up and my hair falls back to my shoulder, I see my mother and father walking toward me ... hand in hand. Their faces are soft and welcoming, and I can almost hear their comforting voices. They move closer and I can hear them calling my name: "Eramane." They speak it softly. I close my eyes and embrace the sound of my parents calling out to me in such a loving way. Even as my eyes are closed, I can still see their images moving closer to me, the light of the sun bouncing off of my mother's braided golden hair. She is so beautiful, and my father holds on to her with a pride that cannot be matched. They are happy and full of life.

They have crossed the meadow and are only a few paces away from me. My mother speaks again: "Eramane, it is not a dream, my love. Wake up." My father grabs my shoulders and restates what my mother has just spoken. He starts to shake me.

"Eramane," he says more sternly, "wake up." His eyes turn from their familiar hazel color. They darken and settle into a deep, bottomless black. My mother begins shouting at me, and now they both have me in their grip.

"What have you done?!" my father shouts.

"You've killed him!" my mother shrieks. They are holding me tightly, and my mother's fingernails are beginning to penetrate my skin. I try to get free of their grasps, but they are too strong. I look at my mother, fear envelops her face. She screams out to me, "It is your fault!" Their faces have changed. They are cold and forlorn. My parents hold me in their grips and continue to scream at me to wake up and redeem myself. Their screams fill the meadow and my ears … like drums beating again and again inside of my head— I can hear nothing else.

CPSIA information can be obtained at www.ICGtesting.com
Printed in the USA
BVOW03s2143060514

352716BV00001B/1/P